FAKE DEATH

A DOTTY SAYERS ANTIQUE MYSTERY

VICTORIA TAIT

KANGA
PRESS

COPYRIGHT

PROLOGUE

The bearded old man shuffled towards the bronze sculpture of a ram, outside the Woolmarket shopping centre, in the elegant Cotswold town of Cirencester.

He whistled a tune he'd heard the Scottish Regiment's pipes and drums play as they paraded through the town centre earlier in the day, and glanced up at the clear blue sky. There was a chill in the air and although he doubted it would freeze tonight, it easily could in another week or two.

There had been some benefits of being in the army. A warm dry place to lay his head and three square meals a day came immediately to mind. The young men and women of the Scottish battalion had marched proudly today, as they should. As he once did.

Still, it had been a good day and he glanced down at the two bulging plastic shopping bags filled with the fruits of his scavenging.

The folk of Cirencester were well-to-do but generous, not like the newcomers from London. He remembered when the Cotswolds was a scattering of small farming communities, but now the area had protected status, like a national park but not as strict, and people with money had moved in and built large houses. They drove around in imposing 4x4s without a smear of mud on them, and ignored the likes of him and those who'd spent their whole lives here.

Wearily, he sat down beside a slumped figure on the base of the ram sculpture, placing his bags carefully by his feet.

"Have a good day, did you?" he joked.

The figure did not respond.

Still, farming wasn't what it was, and the towns and villages were thriving. Even the local schools were full, or so he'd overheard from the conversation of a group of long-haired, stick thin women.

"Haven't you got a home to go to, and a Mrs to cook you Sunday dinner?" He asked the silent figure. Yorkshire puddings. The thought of pancake batter rising and baking into those cup-shaped staples of a roast dinner, filled with succulent slices of beef and a dark, rich gravy, made his tummy grumble.

The immobile figure beside him did not reply, so the bearded man turned to him. "Look mate. It's getting dark and the temperature's dropping. It'll be too chilly for the likes of you out here tonight. So do me a favour, wake up and go home."

He placed his hand on the figure's arm, meaning to shake him awake, and gasped.

The man was not sleeping.

CHAPTER ONE

Twenty-eight-year-old Dotty Sayers hesitated before taking the next step.

She tucked a strand of shoulder-length mousy-blonde hair behind her ear as she looked back at her green Skoda Fabia, parked in a 'Staff Only' parking space. Her hand strayed to the back of her head, and she flinched as she touched the wound, still raw and sore, despite having been inflicted six weeks earlier.

She'd started working at Akemans on a temporary basis for September's Auction, as they'd been shorthanded, but she'd discovered a dead body in a giant grandfather clock.

Piecing together the clues, she'd identified the culprit but realising this, the murderer had tried to silence her - permanently - before she told the police.

Suffering headaches, tiredness, and dizzy spells she recuperated at home but Gilly Wimsey, who ran the antiques section of Akemans, insisted Dotty's temporary job became permanent, but only when she felt ready to start.

Her attention turned to the single-storey stone building in front of her, where a sign above the entrance proclaimed, 'Akemans Auctions'.

The front door opened and a lady with a neat bob of grey hair, immaculately dressed in a tweed skirt and cream polo neck jumper, called, "George told me to look out for you."

Dotty glanced at the adjacent three-storey building, which had once been a flour mill. Hidden in the rolling hills of England's Cotswolds, beside the River Caln, it represented the history of the area, but also regeneration as it had been converted into Akemans Antiques Centre.

To Dotty, it represented a new job. A new start. And hopefully a new life.

"Stop dawdling, it's cold outside," admonished Marion Rook before returning to the auction house.

Dotty shivered as a gust of cool November air brought with it the sweet, rich smell of burning leaves on a bonfire. She adjusted her shoulder bag and walked towards the open door.

"There you are," observed Marion from the back of the office, as she pushed her tortoiseshell-framed glasses up her nose.

The front section of the auction house functioned as both office and reception area. To the left was an open-plan office with two desks, several storage cabinets, and a sink and kitchen units at the back. In front of it was a side door, leading into the adjoining antique centre, and a coat stand stood in the corner.

On the right-hand side there was a seating area, with a grey sofa and tub chairs arranged around an oval reclaimed-elm coffee table. A door from this area led to the main auction rooms, where monthly auctions of antiques, furniture and collectables were held.

Marion poured boiling water into a cup and the aroma of coffee, infused with cardamom, filled the room. "Tea?" she asked in her deep, throaty voice.

"I hope it's OK, but I've brought my own," replied Dotty. "Dr Wimsey suggested I stick to herbal tea at the moment, particularly camomile or peppermint, to ease my headaches." Dotty removed a colourful cardboard box from her bag and handed it to Marion.

Marion's face softened as she regarded Dotty. She removed a tea bag from the box and asked, "Are headaches your only side effects from the attack?"

Dotty took a breath before answering. "I no longer have dizzy spells, which is a relief as it means I'm allowed to drive, but Dr Wimsey warned me I might not be able to stare at a computer for too long, and my focus might wander as I become tired." She smiled slowly, "But I promise, I'll work as hard as I can."

Marion handed Dotty a cup of camomile tea and said, in a businesslike tone, "David and I have agreed to help George with the auctions until the end of the year. Besides, it's too cold for tennis and golf in November and December, and David has no more trips planned until the new year. You only need to do as much as you can handle, although I'm sure Gilly would also appreciate some help in the antiques centre."

The door from the main auction room opened and a tall lady with long blonde hair, and a tailored trouser suit, walked into the office carrying a painting. This was Georgina Carey-Boyd, known to everyone at Akemans as George. She organised the monthly auctions, while her less glamorous, but far more warm-hearted, sister, Gilly Wimsey, ran the antiques centre.

George held the painting up, so it faced Marion and Dotty, and asked, "What do you think?"

Dotty didn't know what to say. She saw a picture of a group of soldiers and an evocative coloured background of blues, reds and yellows. The soldiers' uniforms weren't modern and reminded her of an exhibition of the Battle of Waterloo her late husband, Al, had taken her to.

"Oh, is that a Tom Keating?" Marion's eyes glowed as she stepped forward. "He was a legend in our part of London when I was growing up."

"No doubt he was," George raised her eyebrows, "since he produced and sold many art forgeries. But his own paintings fetch a decent sum these days. This one reminds me of the *Road to Spain* which recently sold for nearly $3,000."

Marion inhaled deeply. "That's quite a sum. If you want to know whether it's real or a fake, I'd ask David." She chuckled. "I think Tom would appreciate the irony, God rest his soul, of other painters forging his work."

"Mrs Carey-Boyd," a male voice shouted from the direction of the auction room.

George sighed. "Our first delivery of the day. I wish we had a porter to organise things, but as we don't, Marion, can you and Dotty check everything has arrived and is intact? We don't want any more missing or allegedly damaged items." She tapped her tailored trouser leg. "I'm leaving shortly for a viewing, so can you also photograph everything and write brief descriptions? Add an estimated value if you can, although David or I will run through the Lots when we prepare November's auction catalogue."

Marion nodded. "Of course." She finished her coffee, returned to the back of the office and washed up her cup. "Ready?" she asked Dotty.

Dotty bit her lip and nodded slowly.

Dotty enjoyed her morning unwrapping items which had been to delivered to Akemans auction house, as she worked alongside the highly efficient Marion.

"Can you find a pair of silver candlesticks on the inventory?" Marion asked.

Dotty put down the lamp she'd partially unwrapped and consulted some stapled pages. "There are three pairs of silver candlesticks on here. Russian silver, Georgian telescopic, and plain silver."

She looked across at the candlesticks Marion had placed on a temporary plastic table and asked, "Which are those?"

"Have a look and tell me what you think," instructed Marion.

Dotty stepped across to the table and paused, before picking up a candlestick. Her brow wrinkled, and she replied in a shaky voice, "It's quite ornate, so I don't think it's the plain silver."

"Correct," confirmed Marion. "But you won't know if the decoration is Georgian or Russian, so the key is the description 'telescopic'. See how the middle section has two different-sized rings, like the tubes of a telescope?"

Dotty peered at the candlestick. "Yes", she replied uncertainly.

"That means it's the Georgian telescopic pair. Take some photographs and I'll write a brief description."

George Carey-Boyd strode across the large room to join them, and asked, "How are you getting on?"

Dotty steadied the auction house's camera and took photos from different angles, as Marion had previously shown her.

"Slowly, but surely," replied Marion. "There are some nice pieces."

Dotty put the camera down and finished unwrapping the table lamp.

Marion turned to George and asked, "What about you? How was your viewing?"

George tapped her foot. "A complete waste of time. The owner only wanted to sell his book collection, which he mistakenly thought was full of rare volumes. I tried to explain that first editions don't always command high prices, particularly if there was a print run in the tens of thousands, but he refused to accept my advice. He said he'd find a specialist dealer, which will just mean wasting someone else's time." She clicked her tongue.

A short lady with an abundance of bright orange curls bustled towards them and grabbed Dotty's arm, saying enthusiastically, "It's great to have you back."

She turned to George and said, "I've just had Aunt Beanie on the phone and she sounds in a real flap."

"I thought she was one of your saner relatives?" remarked Marion dryly. "Despite her appearance. And especially compared with her husband. Do you know he tried to attack me with a pitchfork and accused me of stealing when I collected a picture to be valued last week?" She crossed her arms.

Gilly Wimsey brushed her hair out of her face. "Oh, you mustn't blame Uncle Cliff. Aunt Beanie tries to hide it, but his dementia is getting worse, and I've no idea how she's coping with him, the farm and everything else."

"I've told her numerous times to sell the farm," declared George, "But she's so stubborn, and refuses to."

"A family trait," mumbled Marion.

Gilly smiled sadly at her sister. "You know Uncle Cliff was born there, and he has lived and worked on the farm his entire life. Aunt Beanie thinks it's only fitting he should die there, rather than in some modern house or, worse still, a residential home."

George tapped the ends of her fingers together. "But she can't tie herself to him for the rest of her life. It's such a shame she lost her consultancy job when Gloucestershire's Art and Antiques unit was disbanded. I don't know what she sees in farming. It must be so dull after establishing and running Akemans with father for so long."

Gilly shook her head. "I take my glasses off to her. I know how hard the last two years have been since Fred, their old farmhand retired, and with Uncle Cliff's condition." She turned to Dotty and grinned. "But you should see their house, crammed with a lifetime's baggage. Every cupboard is packed full and any spare corner has a collection of baskets, a pile of boxes or displays of sporting items."

"Typical baby boomer," remarked Marion. "Can't bear to throw anything away. It was the rationing after the war that caused that mindset."

A door opened in the side of the building and a stocky man stepped inside. "Room for another delivery?"

Ignoring him, George asked, "So what does Aunt Beanie want?"

"She muttered something about a priest, donations and a swindling crook. I've no idea what she was talking about, but I think we should pop over."

"I can't," declared George, glancing towards the door as a chair appeared, carried by the stocky man.

"Marion?" enquired Gilly.

"Not likely. I'm keeping well away from your uncle. But why not take Dotty. She's worked hard all morning and I think she should have a break. I don't want to be in trouble with your husband, Gilly, if she develops a headache, or worse still, collapses."

CHAPTER TWO

Dotty sat in the passenger seat of Gilly's little white Toyota Aygo as they drove along narrow Cotswold lanes. It was a bright, but chilly, November day and she thought the orange leaves of a roadside oak tree resembled Gilly's bright hair.

The red and yellow beech hedges gave way to woody-stemmed hawthorn ones and, in the gaps between the hedges, Dotty viewed stubble fields, empty after the summer harvest of wheat, barley and oats.

"It's so beautiful," confessed Dotty as she watched the passing scenery.

"I think the Cotswolds are at their best in spring and autumn," agreed Gilly, as she slowed down and entered a village whose sandy-coloured stone houses were illuminated by the soft autumn light.

"I hope you're not too uncomfortable." Gilly glanced across at Dotty, who'd drawn her knees up towards her stomach in the confines of the car.

"Peter doesn't believe in extravagance, but I'm trying to persuade him we need a family-sized car. The kids are growing and they have so much school kit. Besides, I need space to transport items for the antiques centre, and preferably a vehicle which can cope with the pot-holed lanes I increasingly find myself on when collecting items to sell."

"What about a Land Rover Freelander?" suggested Dotty. "Al's is still standing in the drive and I should really sell it before winter."

Gilly slowed and swerved as they passed two horse riders wearing high-visibility waistcoats. She replied, "But won't you need it?"

Dotty slowly shook her head. "No, I'm happy with my little Fabia. I don't think I could cope with the extra gears and all the complicated functions of the Freelander. If I do trade my car in, I'll keep to something compact and simple."

Black letters on a white metal sign told them they were entering Fairford.

"Aunt Beanie and Uncle Cliff's farm is on the edge of the town, and the farmhouse is coming up on the right," Gilly explained.

They drove through an open gateway, and Dotty noted an old wooden gate slumped against the stone wall of an outbuilding. There were cracks in the concrete yard and a gust of wind picked up a pile of straw and twigs and spun them around in a circle. Dotty shivered.

Gilly laid a hand on her leg. "It'll be warm inside. Come on, it's time to meet my aunt and uncle."

Gilly opened a narrow metal gate and Dotty followed her along an uneven flagstone path between single-storey outbuildings. Inside the house, the entrance area was cluttered with boots and wellies.

Several coats, of varying colours and states of repair, hung on hooks along a wall, while others were piled on an old, frayed armchair. In one corner, it looked as if someone had abandoned an indoor gardening project. Empty plant pots were stacked precariously and a trowel lay on a small wooden table, beside scattered seed packets.

Gilly grinned. "And Peter wonders where my untidiness comes from."

Gilly led them along a terracotta-tiled corridor and Dotty caught glimpses through partially opened doorways of similar chaos in other rooms.

At the far end, Gilly opened an oak door and Dotty blinked as light spilled into the corridor and they entered a large kitchen with a central dining table. At the far end of the room, roof lights and floor to ceiling windows allowed the autumn sunshine to fill the room.

Gilly leaned towards Dotty and whispered, "Building a kitchen extension is the only thing we've persuaded Aunt Beanie to do."

"And it's increased my winter heating bills," said an elderly lady, with white hair and a bright blue headscarf tied with a bow on top of her head. She finished rearranging cushions behind an even older looking man who had wispy strands of grey hair and a toothless scowl.

He jabbed a walking stick towards Dotty and Gilly and shouted, "Intruders. Get out. Out I say."

Aunt Beanie placed a hand on his shoulder. "They're not intruders. That's Gilly, your niece."

"Gilly. No, it's not. She's the little girl with bright red pigtails who cried last week when I caught her and her precocious sister stealing strawberries."

Aunt Beanie picked up a pair of headphones. "Put these on and listen to the farming programme." She placed the headphones on the old man's head and he smiled contentedly.

Aunt Beanie approached them and as she tucked a stray strand of white hair under her headscarf, she apologised. "Sorry about that. He lives mostly in the past these days." She smiled sadly at Gilly and turned towards Dotty. "And who's this?"

Gilly answered, "Dotty Sayers, who's joined us at Akemans."

"How's your head?" asked the older lady as she took Dotty's hands in hers.

"Fine," stammered Dotty as the older woman locked eyes with her.

Gilly asked, "So why were you so worked up this morning that you had to call me?"

Aunt Beanie released Dotty's hands and walked across to the Aga cooker. She lifted one of the heavy, round lids and placed a kettle on the hot plate beneath it. "Take a seat," she instructed.

Dotty sat down at the antique pine table and watched the older lady complete the ritual of tea-making.

"I think someone has made a fool out of me, which isn't something I'm used to, and it's irritating," Aunt Beanie paused, "and embarrassing. And that someone is an imposter priest, of all people."

Dotty was surprised. From Auntie Beanie's appearance, she hadn't expected her to be religious.

"Surprised I'm a churchgoer?" asked Aunt Beanie, handing Dotty a cup of tea. "Ginger with fresh lemon verbena," she added, and Dotty sipped the fragrant tea. "I've kept a plant going, which is one advantage of having the conservatory."

Aunt Beanie returned to the Aga and leaned against it, cradling her own cup, decorated with intertwining flowers.

"St Mary's Church has always been at the centre of the Fairford community. Not only does it host several weekly services, but it runs the local community centre, together with the town council, and organises clubs, activities and events. Besides, your Uncle Cliff was brought up to attend church regularly, and always on high days and holy days."

Gilly turned a chair and sat down facing Aunt Beanie, as she replied, "So surely you know your local vicar?"

"Of course I do," scoffed Aunt Beanie. "But she's not the one who's been visiting us. It was a benevolent man called Reverend Simms, or at least I thought he was, until our own vicar turned up today. She was concerned we'd missed harvest festival, and surprised I hadn't sent my usual selection of jams, chutneys and homemade damson gin."

Aunt Beanie paused, sipped her tea and scowled. "Well, that got me. I'd sent everything with Reverend Simms, and I told her so. And do you know what she asked?"

"Who was Reverend Simms?" suggested Gilly, pushing her orange-framed glasses up her nose.

"That's right. She'd never heard of him and was amazed when I told her the diocese had sent him to visit housebound parishioners."

Aunt Beanie averted her gaze and stared out of the conservatory windows. "She was annoyed, and declared it was her job to visit parishioners who couldn't attend church, and reprimanded me for not calling her."

She leaned back against the Aga and sucked in her cheeks. "I think she felt guilty for not coming to see us earlier."

Dotty asked, in a timid voice, "How long had Reverend Simms been visiting you?"

Aunt Beanie raised her eyebrows. "Good question. About eight weeks. I remember I was pruning the rose bushes and cutting back perennials when he first appeared, and he sat and talked to me in the garden for a while before we went in to see Cliff."

Aunt Beanie's face softened as she looked across at her husband and then stood up.

Dotty watched her settle her husband and placed his headphones back on his head.

"He loves listening to podcasts but doesn't understand that you have to select and play the next episode. He expects it to be like the radio and play continuously." She pulled out a chair and sat at the pine dining table.

"Where was I?" She glanced across at her husband again.

"Ah, yes. Reverend Simms. He was fantastic and listened for hours while Cliff talked about planting and harvesting, and went on about people and animals that are long dead. His visits became regular, on Tuesday mornings and Thursday afternoons, which allowed me time to pop out to do the shopping, or have my hair done," she patted her headscarf, "and I even visited a few friends I hadn't seen since the spring."

She looked down at her hands. "But now it appears he wasn't a real priest at all, and I left Cliff alone in the house with a stranger. And if he stole my harvest festival donation, what else has he taken?"

"Do you still keep the housekeeping money in a biscuit tin?" asked Gilly, raising her eyebrows.

"How do you know about that?" spluttered Aunt Beanie.

Gilly's cheeks flushed. "George and I used to watch through a crack in the door as you filled it, and then George would dare me to take a few pound notes so we could visit the local shop and buy sweets."

Aunt Beanie chuckled. "Well, I never knew about that." She wrinkled her brow. "But I wonder if Cliff did? A few years ago, he persuaded me to only put change in the tin and keep notes elsewhere."

She stood, walked across to a cupboard and reached up to retrieve a square tin with faded pictures of biscuits on it. Returning, she tipped the contents onto the table.

"Only coppers, and some fives, tens and twenties. I'd say someone has removed the pound coins and fifty pence pieces, but it would only have amounted to ten or twenty pounds at most."

"But it does suggest he might have taken other things. Have you had a look?" asked Dotty.

Gilly laughed. "She wouldn't know where to start, and neither would I. I'd feel sorry for any burglar who broke into my house."

Dotty continued in a quiet, sympathetic voice. "But it's not just the stealing, is it? It's the feeling that someone has violated your trust, and the sanctuary of your house."

Aunt Beanie leaned across and put her hand on Dotty's arm. "Is that how you feel about your home?"

CHAPTER THREE

D otty returned home on Monday evening feeling physically rather than mentally tired. Gilly Wimsey had been spurred into action to tidy her office at Akemans Antiques Centre, after their visit to her Aunt Beanie's house.

Dotty had spent the afternoon re-arranging Gilly's bookcase and filing her paperwork. They had started unpacking some of the boxes, which were spread across the office floor, until Gilly decided it was best to tackle them one at a time, log their contents, and either sell items on a stall in the antiques centre, or store them until there was space for them to be displayed.

Dotty wandered around her sparsely furnished military house, which she'd shared with her husband, Alasdair, until he'd died on a military peacekeeping tour less than three months ago. At first, Al's black Labrador, Banff, had kept her company, and they'd taken walks together, but when she was attacked and hospitalised, Al's ex-wife, Angela, had looked after him.

Dotty was uncertain whether she should ask for him back as Angela's children, Zoe and Lucas, loved him dearly and Banff showed them far more affection than he'd ever given her, but she was beginning to feel lonely.

Dotty flinched as the doorbell chimed 'ding-dong'. She opened the front door and found Ian Puck, the regiment's welfare officer, standing on the doorstep wearing a tweed sports jacket and the official tie of 8 SCOTS, The Royal Regiment of Scotland.

"Good, I've caught you at home. The new door bell sounds to be working well, so there'll be no more intruders harming you."

"I don't think they'd necessarily ring the doorbell," Dotty muttered, but Ian did not appear to hear her. He strode into the house and looked around, curling up his bottom lip. "You really shouldn't have let Angela persuade you to sell Al's furniture. Still, perhaps it's for the best." He sighed.

Dotty wrinkled her nose and asked, "Why?"

Ian Puck cleared his throat. "The commanding officer would like to see you tomorrow morning, after the regiment's armistice day parade and two-minute silence."

"Is he making me leave this house?" Dotty's voice was shrill.

Ian pushed his glasses up his nose. "It's complicated, but the CO will explain it all tomorrow. Now don't worry, the regiment will take care of you, and I'll sort out all the paperwork."

Dotty had no idea what that meant, but there was no point asking him until she'd spoken to the commanding officer.

She felt even more dejected after Ian left, and wandered into the breakfast room, stopping beside a vase of blue hydrangeas. She didn't usually buy flowers, but she'd needed something to brighten up the house after the large bouquets the regiment and Akemans had sent had shrivelled up and died.

On Tuesday morning, Dotty parked her Skoda Fabia behind the three-story brick building which housed 8 SCOTS' regimental headquarters. As she climbed out of her car, she heard shouting from the parade square in front of the building, and the resonating stamp of a thousand soldiers standing to attention.

Cautiously, she walked around the building and halted when the parade square came into view. She was always impressed, and intimidated, by the impressive sight of an entire Scottish regiment on parade, wearing their smartest blue and green tartan kilts and ceremonial dress.

Colonel Simon Sutherland, the regiment's commanding officer, stood before his men and women and Dotty thought he was reciting a poem as she caught the words, 'monstrous anger of the guns'.

In the clear air, a lone bugler played *The Last Post* and, as Dotty heard the mournful notes, she felt numb. The last time she'd heard them had been at her husband's funeral. If he'd been here, he'd have been so proud of his regiment and, as he'd told her many times, Scottish soldiers had worn kilts into battle as long ago as Waterloo. She would certainly turn and run if confronted by a savage band of kilted warriors.

Colonel Sutherland stood immobile. He was a tall man and his height was exaggerated by the black cock feather he wore in his glengarry headdress. Even that was an ancient regimental tradition and represented history, honour and allegiance. But had her husband's loyalty and devotion to the regiment led to his death? He'd certainly paid the ultimate price.

As the men disbanded, Dotty left the parade square and entered the headquarter's building, climbing the wide wooden staircase to the first floor. She knocked nervously on the commanding officer's door.

"Come in," an authoritative voice responded.

The room felt airy, and autumn light streamed in through three large sash windows on the outer wall. The cream painted walls were covered with pictures of battle scenes, except on the wooden panels behind a large mahogany desk, which were bare.

Colonel Sutherland removed his glengarry and laid it carefully on his desk. His brown hair was flecked with grey and, when he looked up at Dotty, his dark eyes drew together and he wore a serious expression.

"How are you?" he asked, but rather than wait for a reply he continued, "I'm sorry we haven't taken as much care of you as we should, but the regiment has been rather busy, and then this."

He tapped a piece of paper on his desk. "This news won't be announced until the end of the week, so please keep it to yourself."

He stared at Dotty and she nodded her consent. He continued,

"Our regiment is to be merged with another Scottish one and is returning to Scotland."

Dotty felt herself sway. Colonel Sutherland strode around his desk and pulled a chair out and, gratefully, she sat down.

"I know. The announcement shook me as well, but none of the SCOTS battalions are fully manned and the government has to make financial cuts."

"When?" asked Dotty in a small voice.

The colonel pulled at the sleeves of his dark green wool jacket as he strode back around his desk. He turned and faced Dotty before replying, "They want us to complete the move before Christmas."

Dotty felt numb. She was happy with her new job at Akemans Antiques but now she realised how much she relied on the regiment's support. She knew they would always be there for her if she found herself in trouble … again.

Colonel Sutherland pulled out his desk chair, sat down, and loosely crossed his arms. "I know I said you could have your house for as long as you wanted, which Ian Puck reminded me is unusual for a widow. But I gave you my word, so I feel it is only fair to extend that offer to a property on the new base in Scotland. I can't promise you a house as large as the one you have, but it'll be your own space, and you'll keep the help and support of the regiment and the welfare team."

"Thank you," stammered Dotty.

"And Ian Puck believes he can find you a job in the welfare centre."

There was a knock on the door.

"Come in."

A dark-haired man with an almost comical handlebar moustache, which curled up at both ends, strode into the room.

"Ah, Captain Ward, you're early," declared Colonel Sutherland.

Dotty stood up and stepped towards the door, clutching her hands in front of her.

"Can I introduce you to Dorothy Sayers, whose husband was tragically killed on our recent peacekeeping tour in Africa?"

Dotty looked up at Captain Ward. He was not much taller than her, and he gave her a warm, disarming smile before his expression became serious and he said, "I'm sorry for your loss."

"Captain Ward has agreed to collate a regimental inventory prior to our move, as I suspect many of the treasures will be sold off as surplus to requirements." The Colonel spat out the last words.

"Let's hope not," responded Captain Ward in an upbeat voice.

"Thank you for coming to see me, Dorothy," said Colonel Sutherland, before ushering Captain Ward to the now vacant chair in front of his desk.

CHAPTER FOUR

As the front door of Akemans auction house was locked, Dotty entered the office via the antiques centre. Marion Rook looked up from her computer and regarded Dotty over the rim of her tortoiseshell-framed glasses.

"I thought you'd packed the job in, and that it was too much for you when you didn't arrive earlier."

Gilly Wimsey followed Dotty from the antiques centre.

"I'm so sorry I'm late," apologised Dotty. "I was called to see the commanding officer."

Gilly raised her eyebrows. "That sounds serious. Like being called to see the headmaster at school. What have you done?" She walked across to a collection of keys hanging from a rack on the wall.

"It's not me. It's the regiment," Dotty stammered.

Gilly picked up the chair from the spare desk and placed it in front of the reception desk. "Sit yourself down. All the colour's drained from your cheeks. Marion will make you a cup of tea while you can tell us all about it."

Marion pressed her lips together as she stood up, walked to the back of the office, and switched the kettle on. She turned to face Dotty and asked, "So, what has the regiment done, or not done?"

"They're amalgamating with another regiment and moving back to Scotland."

"Scotland!" Gilly exclaimed. "But that's miles away."

"I know," replied Dotty dejectedly. "And I don't know what to do."

Gilly returned to the key rack and unhooked a set of keys. She leaned against the spare desk and asked, "What did your commanding officer suggest?"

"He said I could move with them. He'd find me a small house and Ian Puck, the welfare officer, believes he can find me a job with the new regiment in the welfare centre or something."

Marion handed Dotty a cup of camomile tea and remarked, "It doesn't sound very inspiring. And what happens when there's a new commanding officer? In fact, if two regiments are merging, will he still be in charge?"

Dotty's hands trembled as she gripped her cup. "I hadn't thought of that."

Gilly tilted her head and observed, in a concerned voice, "I'm so sorry. It's not what you need to hear at the moment. When will they move?"

"Colonel Sutherland said before Christmas."

Gilly's eyes widened. "So soon?"

In a practical tone, Marion stated, "So you have two choices. You can follow the regiment and you'll have a house, and hopefully a job, and their support. But how long will that last? New personnel may forget your husband's contribution, and at some point you'll no longer be their concern, and they'll discard you."

Marion sipped her fragrant cardamom coffee. "Or you can view this as an opportunity, cut your ties with the military, and begin a new life."

Gilly's brow furrowed. "That's easy for you to say, but Dotty's led a sheltered life and she's suffered more than her fair share of knocks recently."

Marion placed her coffee cup on the table, clasped her hands together, and looked down at them. "It's not easy for me to say. I know what it's like leaving an institution, of sorts, and branching out on my own, fending for myself. And I was much younger than Dotty, with none of the social graces she has."

Dotty smiled shyly. "I don't have any social graces."

"You 'ave more 'an a local gal from the East End of London," Marion replied in a cockney accent.

Gilly gasped.

"You see, I've chosen the way I want the world to see me." Marion smiled wryly.

"And what a brilliant job you've done," said a man who resembled a professor, as he entered the office from the auction room. He was not tall, being less than six feet in height, and he had a tanned face with a high, prominent forehead, short grey hair, and a salt and pepper moustache and short beard.

But it was his eyes that made Dotty inhale deeply. They were large and dark and, at the moment, they were playful, like the man's smile, but also watchful.

Marion smiled. "Thank you, David. And we all have our secrets." She raised her eyebrows.

"Good morning, David," said Gilly respectfully as she moved towards the door to the antiques centre and left the office.

"And you must be Dorothy." The man held Dotty's gaze as he inclined his head towards her.

She usually asked people to call her Dotty, but it didn't seem appropriate with this man.

George Carey-Boyd appeared with the painting she'd shown Marion and Dotty the previous morning. "I asked David to look at it, Marion," she sighed. "And he said it is a forgery."

"But it's still a pleasant painting," sympathised David. "We'll describe it as being by an unknown artist, in the style of Tom Keating."

George's shoulders sagged. "But we'll be lucky if it reaches £100. It certainly won't make the four figures a genuine Tom Keating would."

There was silence.

"So Dotty. Are you ready to do some work?" asked Marion.

Dotty stood and replied. "Yes, and thank you for the tea."

"I thought I might take young Dorothy with me?" suggested David Rook.

"What for?" demanded George. "We've plenty of work for her here."

David turned to George and replied soothingly, "My dear

Georgina. If we are to auction the entire contents of Windrush Hall, I believe it will be fitting to do so in situ, and young Dorothy will need to know her way around and distinguish her Rembrandts from her Raphaels."

"If you say so, David," conceded George.

CHAPTER FIVE

D otty sat rigidly in the passenger seat of David Rook's vintage silver Mercedes with the sounds of instrumental music, which made her think of sand, camels, and flying carpets, resonating around her. It was quite a contrast from Gilly's compact Toyota Aygo but she didn't feel any more comfortable.

They turned off the road and onto a drive whose entrance was marked by two stone columns. On the right-hand side there was a single-storey stone cottage.

"That must be the lodge where Norman Climpson lives," David remarked. "He's been the late Duke's groundsman all his life, and his father before him. And when his mother died, some twenty years ago, he took over the housekeeper role as well, although I understand the Duke only lived in a small section of the house. I'm told the old Duke was an exceptional cook," David mused.

"Why are the contents being sold? Surely his heir wants to keep them with the house?" A large Georgian style building came into view in the valley below them. "It's beautiful," whispered Dotty.

"The ancestral home of the Dukes of Ditchford, but now it's for sale," stated David. "The Duke didn't have any family, as he wasn't that way inclined, and his title passes to a distant relative living in South Africa. His lawyers have asked us to look at the contents and give them an idea of their value. Apparently, he hadn't had them appraised, even for insurance purposes, for over fifty years."

They parked in front of a set of wide stone steps leading up to the large front door.

A weather-worn man in his sixties, with an untidy head of hair and an unruly beard, appeared around the corner of the house.

"You'll have to come this way. The front door's warped and I can't open it."

Dotty heard David tut under his breath, but he said in a genial tone, "You must be Norman."

"I am," replied the man curtly.

"And you've managed the whole place on your own?" David's voice held a note of awe.

Dotty watched the wariness retreat from Norman Climpson's features. "The Duke and I got on just fine. We kept to ourselves, but I made sure he was comfortable and he kept me fed and watered."

David Rook joined Norman and as they turned and walked around the side of the house, Dotty heard David remark, "And extremely well, I hear. His suppers were legendary for those lucky few who received an invitation."

The flagstoned kitchen was bright and comfortable and far more modern than Dotty had expected. There was a circular dining table and at the far end several armchairs were arranged around a log burner, set into the fireplace.

A large grey cat jumped down from an armchair and trotted towards them. It stopped several paces away and looked expectantly at Norman.

"This is Earl Grey, the Duke's cat, and he's always hungry."

"He's beautiful," exclaimed Dotty, squatting down on the floor. Earl Grey marched across and rubbed against her legs. "He's so furry, and it's grey, but has a tinge of blue."

The Duke's cat held his head up proudly. He was a large stocky cat, with a flat face and prominent yellow eyes.

"He's a British Blue, which is a pedigree cat, and the Duke joked that he cost the equivalent of a month of my wages. But he kept the Duke company in a no-nonsense manner that he appreciated. I'm not sure what I'll do with him once the house is sold. I'm not a cat man myself."

David Rook strode across the room to a partially hidden staircase and asked, "What's up here?"

"The Duke's bedroom and bathroom," Norman explained. "These were his living quarters. They're not very large, but they are cosy, and easy to maintain."

Norman lifted a large bunch of keys, which had been attached to his leather belt, and searched amongst them. He settled on a brass one, which he inserted into the lock of a heavy oak door at the far end of the kitchen.

Dotty followed Norman through the door and caught her breath. She had stepped into an anteroom of the main house, which lead into the dining room. It was not just the temperature of the house which shocked Dotty, but the feeling of neglect, and stepping back in time.

Sheets, which must once have been white, but were now blackened with dust and dirt, covered the dining table, chairs and other furniture. They even hung on the walls, but one sheet had slipped and the corner of a gilt picture frame poked out beneath it.

David strode across and ripped the sheet away. It was his turn to catch his breath. "Magnificent," he remarked as he stepped back. "The Last Supper. It's not quite Da Vinci, but the colours are still vivid." He turned to Dotty and explained, "Sunlight damages paintings, as it causes chemical reactions in the paint." He turned back to the painting. "Take the vivid blue of Jesus's cloak. Too much exposure to sunlight would turn that a muted grey."

David walked around the room pulling sheets off other pictures, reminding Dotty of a magician revealing hidden treasures. She smiled as he cried with delight. "A Thomas Gainsborough."

Norman appeared unmoved. "A painting of the second Duke, I believe, with his wife and family."

Dotty wandered into the main hall. The dim autumn light glinted dully on the glass chandelier and her footsteps echoed on the stone floor.

Norman followed her, and she asked timidly, "How long has it been like this?"

"Near on sixty years."

Dotty's mouth fell open. "But why?"

"That's not for me to say." Norman shook his head and returned to the dining room, where Dotty spotted him hanging the sheets back on the paintings David had revealed.

The next room Dotty entered must have been a living room, or drawing room she thought the correct term was. She crossed to a window and touched the silk curtains. They were thin, and the fibres parted at her touch, but she dreamed of their former magnificence as she noted their faded embroidery flowers.

David joined her at the window. "The Duke was from a different era, a less tolerant one. I've seen photographs of the parties he hosted here in the late fifties and what amazing, colourful and extravagant events they were. But he was gay, and that was still an offence back then. The local gentry didn't agree with his way of living, so they persuaded the police to intervene and the Duke was arrested, tried and imprisoned."

Dotty heard footsteps approaching and turned to face Norman, who said, "My Dad shut the house up and it nearly broke him. He converted the old kitchen and scullery area for the Duke to live in and the old house fell silent."

"What a waste," muttered Dotty.

"It was. The Duke was an honourable man. Courageous and decorated in battle. But that counted for little amongst the narrow-mindedness and bigotry of the people who lived in these parts. They expected him to hide his true self and wear a mask of respectability, and when he refused, they locked him up."

David prowled around the living room and whisked away several covers, revealing a set of giltwood chairs and two sofas. Dotty ran her hand over the faded silk wallpaper.

David's voice was a mixture of awe and regret as he stated, "This must have been a stunning room with hand-painted peacock blue wallpaper and matching upholstery on the chairs." He squatted down to examine a chair. "I'm surprised. There's no damage or sign of woodworm."

"That's because the Duke insisted I keep the old house clean, dry and vermin free. He even allowed me to hire some of those large blast heaters in winter to prevent the damp seeping in. But he refused to board up the windows, so the sun has done its damage. I tried to protect what I could with the dust sheets."

"This salon suite is worth a bit, even if only for its historical value, and it can easily be reupholstered."

David surveyed the room. "What about the ornaments and silverware?"

"Stored in the old pantry, next to the Duke's living quarters," replied Norman. "The Duke even kept the inventory my parents made when they packed them away."

Dotty felt sad. "Didn't he keep anything to remind him of his old life?"

"Don't get me wrong. He has a small but stunning collection of Cecil Beaton sketches and photographs of the parties and guests who stayed here. He was well-liked and many of his guests were prominent people of the day." Norman lifted his chin proudly.

"And his Victoria Cross?" asked David.

Norman's eyes widened. "You've been doing your homework. Few people remember that."

"Korea wasn't it?"

"Yes, he and my dad were in the 'Glorious Glosters'. They held Hill 235 for two days but in the end they had to retreat and it was a desperate withdrawal. Most of the what was left of the battalion was captured, but the Duke stormed a machine gun post to help his company escape."

Dotty felt cold at the talk of war, but she still asked, "So how did he survive?"

"He was injured in the leg, but my dad pulled, carried and cajoled him to safety." Norman looked down at his hands. "The thing is, he promised me his VC, in memory of my father and as a thank you for our family's service. But I can't find it, or his other medals. They're no longer in his desk where he kept them all these years."

"Has anyone else been in the house?" David asked sharply.

"Only the doctor. He was very good to the Duke and spent hours with him playing chess and discussing the Korean War. He was extremely knowledgeable."

David took a small notebook and pen out of his jacket pocket. "And this was doctor?"

"Dr Rash."

Dotty giggled.

Norman smiled. "Yes, I thought it a fitting name for a doctor and often joked with the Duke about it, especially as the doctor's first name was Hugh. Dr Hugh Rash, or huge rash."

David Rook smiled, but this time it did not reach his large, watchful eyes.

CHAPTER SIX

"Thank you for your time, Mr Climpson," acknowledged David. Dotty shook hands with the unkempt groundsman and felt the calluses on his palms from his years working at Windrush Hall.

She climbed into David's vintage Mercedes and asked, "What will he do?"

"Norman?" queried David, looking back at the retreating figure of Norman Climpson.

"I don't know. What does an uneducated working-class man in his sixties do? What voice does he, and anyone like him, have? And what position do they hold in society? Most of the work they traditionally did is undertaken by machines now. He might find a job as a farm labourer, but there are younger, stronger men for such work. Perhaps he'll end up at the local do-it-yourself store as part of their over-60's training and recruitment programme."

David started the engine and the exotic instrumental music began.

"It must be hard for someone like Norman to start again," mused Dotty.

David turned the music down as he drove away from the house up the long sweeping drive between acres of parkland. "What did you say?"

"I can't imagine him doing that."

"No. I suppose not." David looked across at Dotty as he braked to a halt between the stone entrance columns. "It's a bit out of our way, but would you mind if we visited another prospective client?"

"Not at all. This is fascinating. Does he also live in a large country house?"

"He is a she, and she lives in Chipping Norton."

David drove expertly along the winding roads to the town of Bibury, or basket town, as Dotty thought of it. The main street, known as The Hill, descended to the River Windrush and the narrow medieval bridge built across it. Lining The Hill were numerous shops, cafes, restaurants and pubs, including several shops which, in the summer, displayed wicker baskets on the pavement outside for the many tourists who visited the picturesque town.

After Bibury, David pushed his foot down on the accelerator as the road straightened out and ran across a spine of rolling hills. Branching off it were single-track lanes leading to interestingly named villages such as Bruern, Pudlicote and Ascott-under-Wychwood.

They entered Chipping Norton, a quintessential Cotswold town and, as they passed the neoclassical town hall, with its imposing portico entrance and columns, Dotty remembered a previous visit. Another army wife, who also liked gardening, had taken her to a talk in the town hall about a local award winning garden, which had been designed by three generations of women.

At the far end of the town, David turned into a gravel drive and parked in front of a large, Cotswold stone house with mullioned windows and a steep slate roof.

He knocked on the front door, which was painted a colour Dotty had heard people refer to as duck-egg blue.

A woman wearing jeans and a pink shirt, with her brunette hair tied back in a ponytail, opened the door.

"Mrs Roberts?" inquired David.

"Yes," she replied, standing in the partially open doorway.

David reached into his pocket and withdrew a business card, which he handed to Mrs Roberts. "David Rook, valuer for Akemans Antiques, and my assistant Dorothy." He indicated towards Dotty, who felt her cheeks flush. He made her role sound important and valuable.

The woman smiled and replied, "I'm Sarah Roberts. But I was expecting you earlier."

"Please accept my apologies. We were delayed elsewhere. Would it be more convenient for us to return another day?"

Sarah glanced back into the house and sighed. "No, we might as well get on with it now you're here."

They followed Sarah Roberts along a stone corridor. David stopped and bent down to examine a red Turkish woven rug. "You really shouldn't keep this on the floor. It's far too valuable for people to walk across with dirty shoes."

Sarah shrugged her shoulders. "The stone floor is too noisy without it."

Like Aunt Beanie's house, which Dotty had visited the previous day, the kitchen was light and airy, but huge in comparison with the farmhouse.

A door at the far end opened and a dark-haired man wandered in wearing a white dressing gown and towelling dry his hair. He looked up and froze before proclaiming, "Visitors. I didn't know you were expecting company?"

His accent was foreign and at first, Dotty thought he was Russian, but his pronunciation was softer, so he was probably Eastern European. He wore small, round glasses and had a neat beard and moustache. He reminded her of someone, but she couldn't think who.

"Philip, these people are from Akemans Antiques. They've come to value Freddie's collection, as you suggested."

"That is good. I go get changed and then make everyone drinks. You taste my rakia."

He kissed Sarah on the mouth but, as he left the room, Dotty thought he winked at her.

She was not the only one blushing as Sarah's cheeks were flushed as she blurted, "Philip has been such a comfort to me since my husband's death. I'm not sure how I would have coped without him."

David cleared his throat and suggested, "Shall we get started?"

"Yes, of course." Still flustered, Sarah led them out of the kitchen and across the corridor into the living room, which extended the entire length of the house. Dotty felt as if she'd stepped inside a glossy interior design magazine.

"You have a lovely house," remarked David politely.

Sarah pinched her lips together as she looked around. Mirroring Dotty's thoughts, she replied, "It's like the inside spread of a country house magazine. You can't exactly curl up in here and relax with a book and a glass of wine, or watch the TV."

David picked up a small marble sculpture as Sarah continued, "Everything has its place and Freddie impressed, or bored, many guests with the provenance and value of each item. I hardly dare come in here for fear of breaking something."

David enquired, "You mentioned a rare book collection on the phone?"

"Yes, over here in the glass-fronted bookcase. It's not huge, but Freddie was very proud of it."

Dotty remembered the disdain George Carey-Boyd had had the previous day for a book collection which the owner had said was full of first editions. She was intrigued by David's interest as he squatted beside the bookcase, opened the glass front and extracted a grey book.

He turned it over and whispered, "A 1953 first edition of Casino Royale."

He looked up at Dotty and explained. "See this simple but symmetrical cover design, which resembles a playing card? Ian Fleming designed it himself, and the red hearts on this copy are such a vibrant colour."

"Ah, you like books about spies?" Philip entered the room fully dressed with tan-coloured moleskin trousers and a tweed jacket. "Intrigue and secrets. And now, we try my rakia."

He gave Dotty the impression of someone playing at being an English country gentleman.

"Not for me," replied David, examining another book.

Philip poured dark liquid into a shot glass and brought it across to Dotty. Locking eyes with her, he lowered his voice and said, in a husky tone, "Sip and feel the sensation of the rich, velvety liquid as it slides down your throat."

Mesmerised, Dotty drank.

Sarah Roberts joined them, and with narrowed eyes, commented, "Be careful, it's strong stuff. I'll have a gin and tonic, please, Philip."

Philip turned to Sarah and smiled. "Of course." He left the room.

Sarah turned to David and suggested, "It might be better if you come back another day after all, to see the full collection."

David returned the book he held to the bookcase and stood up.

"Certainly, and if the rest of your late husband's items are like these books, it will be a pleasure, but I think we'll need several days to work through and document the entire collection."

CHAPTER SEVEN

O n Thursday morning, Dotty and David Rook returned to Sarah
Roberts' house in Chipping Norton. It was a wet, blustery day
and David drove carefully across the Cotswolds as the wind and rain
buffeted his car.

Sarah Roberts stood in the corridor of her house and informed
them, "I've prepared a list of items I'd like to sell." She handed David
some stapled sheets of paper.

"That's very efficient of you," he replied. "Where would you like us
to start?"

"In the living room. I'll be in the kitchen if you need me."

Dotty glanced into the kitchen.

Sarah narrowed her eyes and added, "On my own."

Dotty picked up the camera case and laptop bag and followed
David into the living room. He looked at the list before handing it
across to her. "We can use this as our master copy."

She sat down gingerly on a cream upholstered chair and unpacked
the laptop and camera.

"The first item is this French Empire ormolu mantel clock,"
announced David, standing beside the fireplace.

Dotty looked at the list and tapped the item description into her
laptop before carrying the office camera across to David. She searched

the gold statue for the clock face. It was very small and located on the side of a chariot which was being pulled by two rearing horses. "It's very ornate."

David explained, "The clock itself is bronze, and the term French ormolu refers to the process where finely ground particles of gold are gilded onto an object with a mercury amalgam. It enables highly decorative items, such as this clock with its intricate chariot and horses, to be gilded."

"What is it worth?" asked Dotty, as she reached up to touch it.

"In the region of £7,000 to £9,000."

Dotty snatched her hand away.

"We need a more professional method of photographing these items. I have a light box in the car," David told her.

Dotty watched as he entered the corridor and she looked into the kitchen beyond. Would Sarah Roberts mind if she asked for a glass of water? Or, even better, a cup of tea? Her mouth felt very dry.

She tucked a strand of hair behind her ear, drew her lips together and walked purposefully towards the kitchen. She stopped in the doorway as Sarah Roberts looked up from her work at the kitchen table.

"I'm sorry to bother you," stammered Dotty, "but is it possible to get a drink?"

Sarah's face softened. "How rude of me not to offer. My mind is caught up with legal documents this morning."

Dotty stared at Sarah, who wandered across the kitchen and turned the kettle on. In a voice full of awe, Dotty asked, "Are you a lawyer?"

Sarah laughed. "Goodness no. Tea or coffee?"

"Herbal tea, if you have any."

"I was Freddie's PA and sometimes I think he only married me because it was cheaper than paying my wages, or he was worried I'd move and work for someone else."

Emboldened, Dotty asked, "How long have you lived here? It's such a beautiful house."

"Five years. We were in London for ten, but Freddie took on more international clients and he decided they'd be impressed by weekends away in the English countryside during their trips to the UK. So I went from arranging business lunches and dinners in London to weekend house parties in the Cotswolds. Freddie's whole life revolved around his work, or so I thought." Sarah turned away from Dotty and walked towards a pair of patio doors.

Dotty joined her as heavy black clouds parted and a shaft of sunlight illuminated a statue of a Greek or Roman god in the centre of a small pond. It was surrounded by neat beds of bushes with red and yellow leaves and, poking up at the front, Dotty spotted purple autumn crocuses.

Sarah mused, "The garden is my favourite place. I'd no idea how much I'd enjoy being out there, weeding a bed or planting something new and waiting for it to flower."

"I like gardening too," acknowledged Dotty. "But I haven't been able to do more than manage the unruly military gardens that come with our houses."

"Oh, your husband's in the forces?"

"He was," Dotty lowered her head. "But he was killed recently, on a peacekeeping operation."

Sarah touched Dotty's arm. "I'm sorry."

Dotty looked up at Sarah and recognised the pain in her eyes. "What happened to your husband?"

Sarah turned back to the window and stared out into the garden. "He was killed in a diving accident. With his mistress." Sarah's tone was dull rather than angry. "Perhaps I was never more to him than a glorified business employee. He was adamant he didn't want us to have children. What about you?" She turned back to Dotty. "Do you have kids?"

Dotty shook her head. "Al was married before and had a son and daughter, so he didn't want any more."

Sarah turned and walked back to the kettle. "So here we are, two childless widows wondering what to do with our lives. Where do you want to go? What do you want to do?" Sarah turned back to Dotty and her eyes shone.

Dotty shrugged her shoulders. "I've got my job at Akemans, for the moment."

"For the moment?" Sarah opened a cupboard and removed a cup, into which she placed a tea bag.

Dotty looked down at her hands, which were clasped in front of her. "The regiment is moving back to Scotland and if I go with them, I'll have to give up my job."

"Why would you want to move with the army?" Sarah asked, in a confused tone. "Surely you're free of all that now."

Dotty turned back towards the garden and stared out at it. Sarah was right. She didn't have to move with the regiment. She had no duty to do so. But if she didn't, it meant finding somewhere to live, and setting up a life here, in the Cotswolds, with no help from the army.

"I was like you," Sarah admitted.

Dotty turned away from the patio doors and Sarah handed her a cup as she said, "I didn't know what to do when Freddie died. He organised every activity down to the last detail so, when he died, I suddenly found myself with all this time on my hands and no purpose. That's when I met Philip, or Count Philip D'Enliss, as he likes to call himself. We've been to outdoor concerts, the theatre and all variety of sporting events. And I haven't had to look after any clients or organise catering or transport." She grinned. "It's been such fun."

"And what are you going to do now?" Dotty sipped her tea.

"Sell the most valuable items, store the rest, and travel the world with Philip." She eyed Dotty. "But he thinks I'm still a bit stressed and has suggested I attend a wellness retreat this weekend, near Cirencester. I'm not sure I'm into all that woo-woo stuff, but I love the idea of being pampered in the spa. Why don't you join me?"

Dotty started. "Really, but you don't even know me?"

"I can recognise a fellow subjugated wife when I see one. Think about it, and if cost is the issue, let me pay. I've more than enough money. Freddie may have treated me as one of his employees, and had his fun with his mistress, but he was an astute businessman and it appears he used that attribute with his investments and antique collection."

"Are you ready, Dorothy?" asked David from the doorway. "I've set everything up."

Dotty and Sarah exchanged a conspiratorial look and Dotty followed David back to the living room.

CHAPTER EIGHT

Dotty arrived home on Thursday afternoon to find Ian Puck, the regiment's welfare officer, waiting for her.

"Ah, there you are, Dotty. I came to talk to you about the arrangements for Sunday."

Dotty opened her front door and frowned. "Why? What's happening on Sunday?"

"The Remembrance service and parade. I told you about it when you left hospital," Ian replied in an exasperated tone.

"I'm sorry, Ian, but my memory was in pieces back then. You'll have to explain it to me again."

Ian drew his eyebrows together. "As the most recent military widow, you'll lead the parade, behind the regiment's band, and the commanding officer would like you to read a poem in church."

"Me, stand up in front of all those people." Dotty shook her head.

"But it's your duty. In respect for your husband."

Dotty thought of her discussion earlier in the day with Sarah Roberts. She said in a quiet, but firm voice, "I've done my duty as an army wife. Al is dead and I don't want to be paraded around the streets like a campaign prize. I'll join the procession with the other wives or widows, but I'm not doing a reading." She bit her lip and looked down at the floor.

Ian's voice was tight as he replied, "I'm sorry to hear that. The commanding officer will be very disappointed. He told you about the merger, so you realise this is the regiment's final remembrance parade."

Dotty wrung her hands. "OK, I'll walk near the front of the parade, just not by myself. But I'm still not reading in church." Her voice became quiet as she added, "I don't think I can."

As she closed the door behind Ian Puck, her phone rang. She looked at the screen and sighed. It was her father. She drew in a deep breath and answered, in as bright a voice as she could muster, "Hi, Dad. How are you?"

"I've just heard the news about the merger. It's terrible."

"Is it? I thought it was happening to lots of regiments?"

"That's not the point. There is so much history behind the Scottish regiments. But at least you'll be returning to Scotland."

"Dad, I'm not in the army. I'm just a wife whose military husband was killed."

Her father's tone sounded indignant as he responded, "But I spoke to Ian Puck, and he assured me you could move with them and they'd find you a house, and a job, and they'd look after you."

Dotty felt exhausted. "I'm not sure that's what I want."

"Well, come home then. You know you're welcome here. It'll be like old times."

Dotty realised that's what she was afraid of, but she replied, "Thanks. I'll think about it."

On Saturday morning, Dotty turned off the vacuum cleaner. Had she heard the doorbell?

She opened the front door and found Morag MacGill, the regimental sergeant major's wife, huddled on the doorstep with a protective suit carrier draped over her arm.

"Quick, let me in. I'm getting soaked out here," exclaimed Morag, as she picked up a pink sports bag.

In the hall, she handed Dotty the suit carrier and peeled off her raincoat. "It's an angry day out there but hopefully it'll blow itself out, and we're forecast a bright, but chilly day for tomorrow's parade."

She hung her dripping coat on the corner of the dining room door and turned to face Dotty. "So, what were you wearing for Remembrance?"

Dotty shrugged. "I've no idea."

Morag smiled in satisfaction. "I thought as much. Come on, I've a few outfits for you to try on." She picked up the sports bag and climbed the stairs. Dotty followed her with the suit carrier.

In Dotty's bedroom, Morag announced, "Most people will only see your coat, at the parade or in church. Do you have anything else apart from the faded blue one you wore at Al's funeral?"

Dotty shook her head.

Morag unzipped the suit carrier and removed a charcoal grey, knee-length wool coat. "Try this on."

Dotty stood in front of a freestanding, full length mahogany mirror wearing the buttoned-up coat. She stared at her reflection.

"Perfect fit," assured Morag, who stood behind Dotty. "Do you want to wear a hat?"

Dotty bit her lip. "I'm not sure."

Morag tilted her head to one side. "Probably not, and you'll have to take it off for lunch, anyway."

"Lunch?"

"Yes, the principal guests are invited to lunch in the Corn Hall after the Remembrance Service. And that includes you."

Morag swept up the sides of Dotty's hair and held them at the back of her head. "You can't let your hair hang loose, so shall we tie it up with a band or comb, or plait it?"

"I don't think it's long enough to plait, and anyway I can't do that by myself."

"I could do it for you in the morning when Fergus and I pick you up."

"Pick me up?"

Morag sighed. "What did Ian tell you?"

"That I'm to take part in a parade and there's a church service."

"Did he tell you where?"

Dotty locked eyes with Morag in the mirror. "No. Isn't it in the village?"

"No. The parade is through the centre of Cirencester and the service is at St John Baptist church, on Market Place."

"I'm glad I refused to do a reading. There's no way I could stand up in front of all those people."

Morag raised her eyebrows and muttered, "So that's why Ian only asked me yesterday if I'd read a poem."

Dotty gulped and considered her reflection. "I have a red bow I could secure my hair with," she suggested in an overly bright tone.

Morag nodded. "OK, and I can always fix it, if needed, tomorrow. Now your neck. Do you have a scarf?"

"Yes," exclaimed Dotty. "I bought one with poppies on, especially for Remembrance, when Al and I visited the home of the Chelsea Pensioners in London." She routed about in her bottom drawer and withdrew the scarf. Attached to it was a knitted poppy.

"Oh, look. I bought this at the spring bazaar in the welfare centre. The young girl on the stall was very earnest as she told me how she'd learned why the poppy symbolises Remembrance and all the soldiers who've died in war. She even recited the first verse of the poem, Flanders Fields, and explained how poppies grew on the battlefields after World War One." Dotty stood in front of the mirror and fastened the poppy to the coat, on the left side.

"Are you really going to wear that? It's a bit … homemade."

Dotty tilted her head to one side. "Exactly. There's something personal about it."

Morag drew her lips together before asking, "Where are Alasdair's medals?"

"In a box, next door. Why?"

"As his widow, you are entitled, and expected, to wear your husband's medals. Fetch them and we'll attach them to your coat, so you're all ready."

Dotty left the room feeling more like she was putting together a costume for a play. Al had won the medals, not her, but she was still expected to play the part of the grieving widow.

CHAPTER NINE

On Sunday morning, Dotty stood in a large car park in the historic town of Cirencester, and lifted her head to the catch the warming rays of autumn sunshine.

All around her, preparations were underway for the forthcoming parade. The regimental pipers blew into their bagpipes and the drummers lifted the straps, which held their instruments in place, over their heads.

"Nice day for it," a man's voice declared.

She lowered her head and locked eyes with Captain Anthony Ward.

There was something disarming about him. "Have we met before?" she asked.

"Don't you remember, in Colonel Sutherland's office?"

"No, I mean besides that."

"You know what the army is like. People are always bumping into each other in different places."

She drew her eyebrows together. Was that it? Had they met in Scotland or at a military event?

She looked more closely and realised he was wearing a brown uniform with a black peaked cap. A string of medals adorned his jacket.

Captain Ward leaned closer and confided, "I'm with the Rifles, not Scots. Mind you, I've always wondered what it's like to wear a kilt. Do you think it gets a bit chilly, you know, down below?"

Dotty giggled.

"Are you ready?" asked Colonel Sutherland as he approached, wearing his kilt and tucking his ceremonial knife into the top of his sock. A large sword hung down from his leather cross belt.

Dotty turned to him and replied, in a hesitant voice, "Yes."

"Good, you'll join me and my wife at the front of the parade, behind the pipes and drums."

Dotty turned back to Captain Ward, but he had disappeared.

She took her place in the procession, to the left of the commanding officer, as the shrill sound of the band's pipes began to play. It was a haunting but emotional sound and as Dotty stepped forward, in line with Colonel Sutherland, she had the first inkling of what it must feel like to be a soldier in the regiment, to be part of the clan.

She felt proud and held her head high as they marched slowly through the streets. She might not be a serving soldier, but she was still part of the military family.

Someone in the crowd called her name and waved. She glanced across and recognised the smiling face of Sarah Roberts. Wasn't Sarah supposed to be on a wellness retreat?

Spectators on both sides clapped as they marched through Market Place and drew to a halt outside the impressive, gothic, stone entrance porch of St John Baptist church. Colonel Sutherland ushered Dotty inside.

The service was poignant, but she was too embarrassed to wipe away the tears which dripped down her face when she sang the hymn, 'I vow to Thee, my country'. But as she knelt to pray, she heard snuffles and nose blowing around her and realised she wasn't the only person crying.

After the service, she stood outside, beside the gothic bell tower, and gratefully inhaled the fresh November air.

Morag MacGill patted her arm. "Are you coming to lunch?"

Dotty walked beside Morag and said, "Well done with your reading. It wasn't an easy poem."

"No, it wasn't. And I'm pleased it's over." Morag held her hand out in front of her. "Look, I'm still shaking. I need a glass of wine."

They walked under the stone entrance arch into the Corn Hall arcade. A restaurant was open with a few early Sunday diners and, once again, Dotty spotted Sarah Roberts, who was seated with a group of women near the window. She smiled up at Dotty.

"A friend of yours?" asked Morag.

"Someone I've been doing some work for," replied Dotty, noncommittally.

The rest of the shops were closed, but Dotty heard a loud hum of chatter up ahead. They passed the entrance to a small hall where table stalls were set up selling vegetables, cakes and various homemade jams and chutneys.

Morag followed her gaze. "It looks like a farmer's market. I might pop in later."

They continued through to a hall at the end of the arcade where people stood in groups, between tables laid for lunch, talking and sipping their drinks.

A soldier, who held a tray of glasses, asked, "Drink, Ma'am?"

"Prosecco, just what I need. Here, Dotty." Morag passed Dotty a tall glass of sparkling wine and, spotting someone across the room, added, "I'll be back in a tick."

Dotty gazed around the room at all the relaxed, chattering people.

An older man in his sixties caught Dotty's eye and approached her. "You're the lady from Akemans, aren't you? Who came to Windrush earlier this week?"

Dotty started and asked, "Mr Climpson?"

He snorted. "I see my appearance has confused you."

It had. The man in front of her was clean shaven and his sandy hair was cut short. As she looked closer, she realised he had the broken veins and permanently tanned face of someone who'd spent the majority of their life outdoors.

"Did you serve in the military?" she asked politely. He had a line of medals on the right of his jacket and above them, an attractive enamelled poppy with an emblem of a sphinx.

Norman rubbed his chin. "I would have liked to, and followed in my father's footsteps, but I was needed on the estate. A strong young pair of hands and all that."

Dotty was uncertain what to say next.

"You're probably wondering what I'm doing here."

Dotty nodded.

"The old Duke was always invited and lately I've accompanied him. We were still sent an invitation, so I thought I would come along. Pay my final respects to the Duke and my father before I move on."

Dotty sipped her drink. She would prefer something soft but didn't like to leave Norman by himself, or find herself on her own again.

"What will you do?" asked Dotty.

"I don't know. And it's not just a job. I need to find somewhere to live as well."

Dotty could relate to that. She needed somewhere else to live. But was it in Scotland, with the regiment? She looked around at the people again. She just didn't feel like one of them.

Dotty jumped as someone tapped her arm.

"Sorry, didn't mean to startle you." Gilly's Aunt Beanie stood next to Dotty, wearing a bright red headscarf and a long bulky red cardigan, with a jolly jewelled ladybird brooch. "I saw you walk past and wondered if you'd invite me to lunch. There's been a tantalising smell of curry all morning, and my sandwiches have curled up in shame."

"Er, I'm not sure," faltered Dotty. She noticed the clasp of Aunt Beanie's brooch was undone and the ladybird was hanging down.

"Excuse me," she said and hooked it back into place.

"Thank you."

"I would be delighted to accompany you to lunch," declared Norman Climpson.

"Marvellous. And a veteran to boot."

"Alas, no. I'm wearing these to honour my father, who served in the Second World War and Korea, and my former employer and friend, the Duke of Ditchford."

Aunt Beanie leaned forward and screwed up her eyes. "Where is the VC? The Duke was such a valiant man, and yet he was still shunned by polite society."

Norman looked down at his feet. "That medal, the pride of his collection, is missing."

"Missing? As in lost or stolen?" exclaimed Aunt Beanie. Several people, standing close to them, turned their heads.

"Yes," admitted Norman.

"Well, which is it?" Aunt Beanie pressed.

"I don't know." Norman's voice dripped with shame.

Aunt Beanie clasped Norman's elbow. "Let's have lunch and we can devise a plan to find it."

They joined the lunch queue and Aunt Beanie remarked. "Every British institution is the same. They love their queues." She turned to Norman Climpson and held her hand out. "Bernadette Devereux, but everyone calls me Beanie."

"Norman Climpson."

As they shuffled forward, Dotty looked back at Aunt Beanie.

"You want to know what I'm doing here?" Aunt Beanie's eyes sparkled.

Dotty's cheeks flushed.

"Perfectly understandable. I'm serving my penance to the church and helping at their stall at the farmer's market next door." She turned to Norman. "You must come and try my Damson gin after lunch."

Norman smiled, "I'd be delighted to."

Dotty passed a pleasant lunch, listening to Norman and Aunt Beanie discuss past and present events in the Cotswolds.

Captain Anthony Ward sat a few tables away with people Dotty did not know. He raised his head and smiled at her.

"Who's that?" enquired Aunt Beanie.

"Captain Ward. He's preparing an inventory of the regiment's valuables."

"He looks vaguely familiar." Aunt Beanie scowled.

Norman turned towards Captain Ward, who bowed his head. "I agree, but I can't think why."

Morag MacGill approached their table, sat down, and extended her hand. "Hi, I'm Morag."

"Beanie," said Aunt Beanie as she bit down on a poppadom.

Norman shook the proffered hand. "Delighted to meet you, I'm Norman Climpson."

Morag turned back to Dotty. "I have to stay to help clear up, but the commanding officer's wife has offered you a lift home. Is that OK?"

Dotty gulped and nodded, but her hands felt sweaty. "Do you mind if I leave you?" she asked Norman and Aunt Beanie.

Aunt Beanie shooed her away with her hand. "Norman and I need to plan our campaign to find the Duke's VC, which I think we should do over a glass of damson gin."

All four of them stood, and as Dotty followed Morag MacGill, she glanced back at Aunt Beanie and Norman Climpson as they passed Captain Ward's table.

CHAPTER TEN

O n Sunday evening, Dotty didn't feel like eating supper after the substantial curry the regiment had provided for lunch, following the Remembrance parade. She changed into a comfy pair of Al's pyjama bottoms and an old jumper, and curled up on her favourite wing-backed chair in the living room. Cradling a cup of camomile tea, she switched on the TV.

The news programme showed the Prime Minister laying a wreath at the Cenotaph in London and then it cut to clips from Remembrance parades around the country.

"And now to our reporter in Cirencester."

Dotty started and sloshed hot tea on her pyjamas. She watched in fascination as she saw herself, next to the commanding officer, march past the camera, behind the pipes and drums.

"But the final Remembrance parade for this historical regiment was marred by the discovery of a man's body an hour ago. The police have not released his identity, but he is believed to be wearing military uniform and to be in his mid-forties. His body was discovered by an elderly man, slumped against the Woolmarket ram sculpture, in a lane leading off the central marketplace. There is considerable police activity at the moment and speculation that the man did not die from natural causes."

"Get out of here," shouted a disgruntled Welsh voice. "Don't you know this is a crime scene?" Dotty recognised the deep, melodic Welsh voice of Inspector Evans, shouting at the reporter.

The news programme returned to the studio.

Who was the dead man? If he was in his mid-forties, he was likely to be an officer or senior soldier. One of Al's friends? And possibly someone she knew.

She went upstairs to change her pyjama bottoms and when she returned the opening sequence of The Antiques Tour was playing, so she settled down to watch it, trying not to think about the dead man in Cirencester.

When Dotty arrived at Akemans on Monday morning, she was surprised to find Gilly Wimsey already in the office. She was leaning over the front desk, reading a newspaper with Marion Rook.

She looked up at Dotty and cried, "Isn't it terrible? This poor man who was murdered in Cirencester yesterday."

"He was definitely murdered?" asked Dotty as she hung her coat on the stand in the front corner of the office.

Marion tapped the newspaper. "That's what it says here." She eyed Dotty over the top of her tortoiseshell-framed glasses. "Weren't you in Cirencester yesterday?"

Gilly nudged Marion in the side. "How can you think Dotty had anything to do with it?"

"I don't," scoffed Marion. "But she might have spoken to the man, or seen him."

With a sombre tone, Dotty replied, "I saw lots of people at the parade yesterday. But I only spoke to a few of them. Does the paper say who the dead man was?"

Marion shook her head. "That's the queer thing. He had no identification on him. No phone. No wallet. No keys."

"Do they think he was robbed and then killed?" asked Gilly.

"The paper says the police are considering it as a possibility, and are appealing for witnesses." Marion turned the paper over. "Look, here's a sketch of the man." She turned the paper towards Dotty.

Dotty stepped closer and drew her eyebrows together as she stared at the photograph. The man was familiar, but the image troubled her, as if it was a composite of different faces.

"He looks very ordinary to me," commented Gilly, as she stepped around the desk and stood next to Dotty. "I suppose he could be handsome, but it's difficult to tell."

The door to the auction room opened and George Carey-Boyd swept into the office. "Excellent, you're all here."

Gilly looked up. "You insisted I come in early today, even though Peter acted the martyr about taking the kids to school this morning. He put his hand on his breast and quoted something about being deeply wounded, and clearly his time was less valuable than mine."

"How did you respond to that?" asked Marion, raising her eyebrows.

"I threw a shoe at him as I left."

"Never mind that," dismissed George. "It's less than two weeks until our next auction. What items are still to be delivered?"

Marion tapped the keys on her computer. "I've entered everything we have so far on the system and in the auction catalogue document." She studied her screen and added, "So tomorrow, we have a delivery from the house in Chipping Norton that David and Dotty have been itemising, and a firm of receivers are dropping off tables, chairs, and other equipment today from a restaurant they closed down. And that's everything for this month's auction."

Marion removed her glasses and looked up at George. "I have to send the finalised catalogue to the printers by closing time on Thursday."

"When did Sarah Roberts decide to go ahead with the sale of her husband's collection?" asked Dotty timidly.

"She sent me a message on Friday afternoon," replied George. "David is delighted and said the pieces are valuable and great care has been taken putting the collection together. It should draw considerable interest, from London and internationally." George had a satisfied look as she crossed her arms.

Marion continued. "David is meeting Mrs Roberts this morning to finalise the items being sold, and then Vintage Removals are packing and transporting them, as the collection is too precious to trust to our usual removal guys."

"Anyway, Shaun and Justin are busy working for me. Which brings me to my next point," announced George. "We need a full-time porter, and preferably before next week's sale."

Gilly muttered, "At last. My arms are aching from all the fetching and carrying in the antiques centre."

"What's that?" demanded George.

"Why don't we advertise in the *Cirencester Gazette*?" suggested Gilly, looking sheepish.

George pursed her lips. "We need someone we can trust one hundred and ten per cent. And we can't expect someone like that to just walk in off the street."

Gilly winked at Dotty, and turned back to George. "Like Dotty."

George tapped her foot. "You know what I mean. But we need a man ..."

"Or woman. I don't think you can suggest that women are less strong or able than men for the role," Gilly interrupted with a holier-than-thou tone.

"It doesn't matter," snapped George. "We just need someone capable of carrying furniture, repairing broken items and undertaking general maintenance. Preferably someone young and fit."

"I've seen some young fit men coming in and out of that new gym on Dyer Street in Cirencester," mused Gilly.

"Gilly, will you shut up," screamed George. "This is serious. I need you all to ask around and try to find someone suitable for the role. But I repeat. They must be completely trustworthy. We don't want any more allegedly damaged or missing items."

As Gilly and Marion moved towards the back of the office, Marion whispered, "That'll rule out most of your fitness guys."

Gilly giggled. "One can but dream."

The phone rang.

"Dotty, can you answer that?" asked Marion.

"Good morning, Akeman Antiques," said Dotty as she picked up the receiver.

"Good morning, this is Colonel Sutherland. I believe Dorothy Sayers works with you."

Dotty's stomach lurched. At least the commanding officer was still alive, but what did he want with her?

"Hello sir, this is Dotty."

"Oh good. Now this is rather a delicate matter. My superiors want an itemised inventory of all the silverware, collectables and paintings in the officers' and sergeants' messes by the end of the day, two weeks from today, so I wondered if one of your colleagues could undertake the task."

"But I thought Captain Ward was doing that?"

"He was," confirmed Colonel Sutherland, "but this is now official business, and we need an expert to value the items. Besides, Captain Ward hasn't arrived this morning."

CHAPTER ELEVEN

On Monday afternoon, Dotty followed David Rook into Colonel Sutherland's office.

The Colonel looked composed as he shook hands with David and said, "I really appreciate you coming at such short notice." He handed a list to David. "A territorial officer, Captain Ward, has made a start with the inventory and I hoped he'd be here to discuss it with you. But it probably doesn't make any difference, since we need the collection valued by a professional firm. That's why I asked for your help."

David turned and surveyed the room.

Dotty followed his gaze across the paintings on the wall, which depicted different battle scenes.

David walked across to one which hung above a sideboard. "Iraq?" he enquired.

"Yes, the Gulf War. Painted by an artist who specialises in modern military scenes."

The setting was a desert, and the picture depicted soldiers, including one playing bagpipes, standing beside a tank, surrounded by palm trees.

David picked up a curved dagger and slid the blade out of its sheath.

Colonel Sutherland explained, "I bought that from a lady begging outside the camp gates when I was serving in Iraq. My interpreter told me her husband had been shot, and she was left to fend for herself and her four children. Unfortunately, that was a common story, so I bought the dagger from her and hoped she'd be able to feed her family for a while. The sheath's only embossed metal over wood and the stones aren't precious."

David wrinkled his nose as he slipped the Iraqi dagger into its sheath and placed it back on the sideboard.

Colonel Sutherland walked across to the panelled wall behind his desk and inserted a key into a discrete lock. A door in the panelling swung open.

"We keep items not on display, or only used for dinner nights, in here."

Dotty walked across to the hidden room and stepped inside. Floor to ceiling shelving covered three walls and a box of what Dotty presumed were paintings, because of their bubble-wrapped shapes, was pushed against the fourth wall, beside the door. Intrigued, she picked up a rectangular black case from the shelf beside her and opened it. Inside was a crystal decanter with a silver stopper in the shape of a horse's head.

From the next room, Dotty heard David ask, "Apart from this room, and the ante-room, where else are there items for us to add to the inventory?"

"The Officers' and Sergeants' messes contain paintings and silverware, and you'll find various items on display here, in the headquarters building. I'll ask the lieutenant in charge of possessions to show you around. He's knowledgeable about regimental history and can explain the provenance of many items," replied Colonel Sutherland.

Dotty heard another voice. The deep, melodious Welsh voice of Inspector Evans, who enquired, "Colonel Sutherland?"

"Yes, and who are you? And why do you think you can walk into my office unannounced without knocking?" Colonel Sutherland's voice remained calm but authoritative.

There was a pause before the inspector responded. "This warrant card gives me permission, it does. And you are?"

"David Rook."

"And what do you have to do with the military?"

David's tone had a touch of humour as he replied, "Absolutely nothing. I'm here at Colonel Sutherland's request, to value some regimental items."

"Fair do's. But would you mind leaving so I can speak to the Colonel?"

Raising his voice slightly, David responded, "I'll wait outside."

Dotty was trapped in the anteroom, but she was intrigued to know why Inspector Evans was here. Was the man who died in Cirencester from the regiment?

Inspector Evans began, "I'm sure you've heard that a man's body was discovered in Cirencester yesterday evening. And as he was wearing a military uniform, I presume he was part of your parade. But he wasn't wearing a kilt, and you haven't reported anyone missing."

"First, kindly have the courtesy to introduce yourself," instructed Colonel Sutherland.

"Inspector Evans."

"Well, Inspector. We held a full regimental muster this morning and I can confirm nobody is missing from the battalion."

There was a pause and a rustling sound before Inspector Evans responded, "We found this business card in a wallet, close to the body. Your business card."

"So you think I knew the dead man?"

"I do." There was another pause and then the inspector said, "Have a look at this photograph. I'm sure you've seen dead bodies before and won't be squeamish."

There was a brief silence. "The man does look familiar, but I can't place him. Who did you say he was?" The colonel sounded unperturbed.

"I didn't, but his credit cards are in the name of Anthony Ward."

Dotty recoiled and knocked against a shelf. A box fell off and hit the floor with a clunk.

"Who's that?" growled the inspector.

Keeping her eyes on the floor, Dotty left the anteroom and entered the office.

"I'm not being funny, but why were you hiding in that cupboard?"

"I wasn't hiding. I just happened to be in there when you arrived." Dotty bit her lip and looked up at the inspector.

"You? I suggest you stop skulking around in cupboards and keep your nose out of police business if you don't want to end up in hospital again."

Dotty bowed her head and glanced across at the photograph on the colonel's desk. It was a face, one she half recognised and with a sudden insight she picked up a pen and scribbled a comical moustache, which curled up at the ends, on the photo.

"That's it, that is. I'm arresting you for interfering with police evidence," declared the inspector.

Colonel Sutherland said levelly, "Just a minute, Inspector." He examined the photograph again, and his dark eyes widened, but only slightly.

Inspector Evans scowled at the colonel. "Recognise him, do you?"

"Yes, it is Captain Ward, who's been working here producing an inventory of the mess paintings and valuables."

So she had known the dead man, and she'd spoken to him before the Remembrance parade. But who would want to kill him? She leaned against the desk and gulped down air.

"You all right, are you?" The inspector's tone was put out rather than concerned.

Dotty shook her head. "I knew Captain Ward, and I spoke to him yesterday."

Colonel Sutherland sounded unmoved as he said, "The two of them met in this office, last week."

"I'll ask Constable Varma to take your statement, when you've safely returned to Akemans. Now, if you don't mind, I'd like to continue my discussion with Colonel Sutherland. Alone."

Dotty glanced across at the Commanding Officer who remained composed as she walked out of his office.

CHAPTER TWELVE

Dotty was the first to arrive at Akemans on Tuesday morning. The weather was dull and blustery and the dark gathering clouds threatened rain. She remained in her little Skoda Fabia until a maroon coloured removal lorry pulled up in the gravel yard. Two men climbed down and walked towards her car.

Hesitantly she got out and struggled to pull on the charcoal-grey wool coat Morag MacGill had lent her, and she hadn't yet given back.

"Morning, miss. Do you work here?" one of the men asked.

Dotty gulped before replying, "I do, but I'm afraid I don't have the keys to open up."

At that moment, a silver VW Golf drove into the yard and parked neatly beside Dotty. Marion Rook climbed out wearing a black bucket hat and a matching padded jacket.

"Good morning," she called, as she approached the lorry men. "Are you from Vintage Removals?"

"That's right. And we have some crates for you. Where would you like us to put them?" the closest man asked.

Marion responded, "Do we have to unpack everything now, or can we keep them in their crates until next week?"

The man turned to his colleague, who shrugged. "I suppose there's no harm in keeping them until next week. If you put all the packing material back in the crates and give us a call when you're ready, we'll get someone to collect them. But don't you have an auction next week?"

"We do," agreed Marion.

"At least one client usually asks us to collect a piece of furniture they've bought, so the driver can pick the crates up at the same time. Now, where shall we put them?"

"Come with me. You too Dotty. We'll store everything in the secure room in the antiques centre until after the weekend. Dotty, can you check the box numbers and sign off the delivery?"

Dotty shrank back but replied, "I suppose so."

"Good girl."

Dotty followed Marion and spent the next hour ticking off crate numbers and randomly unwrapping bundles to make sure the contents matched those written on the inventory she held.

When she returned to the office, Marion said, "Now I'll show you how to put together the auction catalogue."

Dotty tried to concentrate on everything Marion told her, but her gaze kept wandering across to the door to the antiques centre. Perhaps the inspector no longer needed her statement and wouldn't send Constable Varma to collect it. But that meant she wouldn't learn if any progress had been made in the inquiry into Captain Ward's death.

By four o'clock, Dotty's head hurt and she kneaded her forehead as the door to the antiques centre opened.

"Is my patient disobeying doctor's orders and working too hard? That won't do, it won't do at all."

"Dr Wimsey," quipped Marion. "Dotty is not your patient. Anyway," she said in a resigned tone, "she hasn't much work left to finish." She picked up her bag and left the office.

Dr Wimsey watched her retreating back and commented, "A tough lady and a hard taskmaster, but between my shambolic wife, and her highly strung sister, things would fall apart round here without her." He looked keenly at Dotty. "She's a hard act to follow, don't you know?"

Dr Wimsey unzipped his lightweight waterproof jacket and hung it, together with his cycling helmet, on the coat stand in the corner. Underneath, he wore Lycra cycling leggings and a light-blue fleece jumper.

Dotty raised her eyebrows and asked, "Do you cycle to visit your patients all year round?"

"If I can. What's good for the heart is good for the head, but bicycles and black ice are not natural soulmates, and fresh snow is too stubborn."

Dotty wrinkled her brow and asked, "Have you come to see Gilly? I think she's in the antiques centre."

"Actually," he replied in a serious tone, "while you are not officially my patient, I still have a duty of care for your wellbeing. I popped in to make sure Mrs Rook was not cracking the whip too regularly."

Dotty smiled ruefully. "She's been very patient, but I have struggled to understand how to put the auction catalogue together this afternoon. I feel as if I'm wading through fog to find the words I need, and the energy." She leaned back in her chair.

Dr Wimsey scrunched up the corner of his mouth. "I'm going to blow the whistle and call full-time on your work today."

The door to the antiques centre opened and a black-hatted head appeared. "Hiya," called Constable Varma.

"Ah, the local constabulary has arrived. What news of the deathly case in Cirencester? Has the corpse been identified? And was he a double-dealing villain or a pillar of society?"

Constable Varma removed her police hat and patted her dark hair, which was secured in a bun at the nape of her neck.

"He was an army officer," revealed Dotty.

"Actually," began Constable Varma, before clamping her mouth shut.

"Ah ha," cried Dr Wimsey. "I taste the salty tang of intrigue." He leaned towards Constable Varma. "Serve up all the juicy details."

"I can't," replied the constable with a pained expression.

Dotty said softly, "I was with Colonel Sutherland when he identified Captain Ward, and I also recognised the victim. Was I wrong?"

Constable Varma slowly shook her head. "Not exactly."

Dr Wimsey grabbed the chair Marion had been using and set it down in front of Dotty's desk. With a sweeping gesture, he announced, "Take a seat my uniformed compatriot, and lay out this web of intrigue before us."

Constable Varma sat down and pursed her lips. She looked from the expectant Dr Wimsey to Dotty.

"Ok, but promise you won't tell anyone."

"Not a soul," declared Dr Wimsey.

"There was no identification on the body, but one of my colleagues found a wallet discarded in a dustbin, not far from where the body was found."

"Was that the one with Colonel Sutherland's business card in it?" asked Dotty.

Wide-eyed, the constable responded, "It was. And there were several credit cards in the name of Anthony Ward."

"What did I tell you?" Dotty sat up, smiling in satisfaction.

Dr Wimsey was watching Constable Varma. "I suspect this matter is not so easily unravelled. Am I right?"

Constable Varma looked up at him. "You are. We traced Captain Ward's address to a semi-detached house on the main Oxford Road leading into Swindon, near the retail park."

Dotty frowned. That didn't sound like the kind of place where an army officer would live.

"But we discovered the house was rented by a Todd Mountebank."

"A swindler by name, a swindler by nature, no doubt," announced Dr Wimsey.

Constable Varma swung round in her chair and accidentally kicked Dr Wimsey. "So sorry," she gasped, "but why did you say that?"

Dr Wimsey rubbed his leg and replied in a strained tone, "The definition of 'mountebank' is a person who deceives others in order to obtain money."

Dotty regarded Dr Wimsey shrewdly. She was certain that beneath his nonsensical comments and his tomfoolery, there was a sharp mind.

Constable Varma fiddled with her hat as she confirmed, "The man who rented the Swindon house was called Mountebank, and he moved from London five years ago."

"And was Captain Ward renting a room from him?" enquired Dotty.

Dr Wimsey leaned back. "I don't think so."

Again, Constable Varma looked up at him with wide eyes. "No, Captain Anthony Ward and Todd Mountebank were the same person."

Dotty's head throbbed.

CHAPTER THIRTEEN

"Good Morning," said Marion in a matter-of-fact tone, on Wednesday morning, as Dotty entered the auction office at Akemans Antiques. "I'd like to introduce you to Jordan. He's come to try out for the porter's job."

Dotty smiled at the young man, but his head was bowed over his phone.

"His mother is my cleaner, and she said he needs something useful to do to get him away from his computer."

"And we've plenty of work for him here," added a breathless Gilly Wimsey, who had followed Dotty into the office. She scraped a hand through her unruly orange curls and announced, "George wants us to start arranging furniture in the auction room today."

"We don't normally start that until the Thursday before an auction," replied Marion with a pinched expression.

"I know, but we'll be busy next week arranging the valuable Chipping Norton collection." Gilly turned to the young man and asked, "Jordan, is it?"

He looked up at her and nodded before returning to his phone.

"Put that away and follow me," instructed Gilly. In a softer tone, she added, "I'll show you our storeroom."

As Gilly led Jordan away, Marion turned to Dotty. "You need to add the Chipping Norton collection to the catalogue, as I showed you yesterday. Did David give everything an estimated value?"

"There were a couple of items he wanted to research further."

"You can ask him about those later, as he's at the military barracks this morning. He wanted to take you, but I told him we had too much work here. I hope you don't mind, but we have to complete the catalogue and you helped him assess the items Sarah Roberts is selling."

Marion joined Gilly and Jordan in the main auction room, so Dotty was able to enjoy having the office to herself. She made a cup of chamomile tea, found the notes and photographs from her visit to Sarah Roberts' house, and began to input the information into the auction catalogue.

She was occasionally interrupted by Gilly or Marion, making cups of tea and coffee, and they sent Jordan in several times to check Lot numbers for various items.

Early in the afternoon, Jordan carried two pine stools into the office. "Mrs Rook said these are with the restaurant clearance items, but she's not sure which Lot."

Dotty smiled at him and replied, "Let me check."

She tapped her keyboard and asked, "How are you getting on?"

He plonked a stool on the floor and sat on it. "It's hard work. I've spent all day lugging furniture about and I only had half an hour break for lunch. By the time I got logged onto my game, it was time to start work again."

After Jordan left, Dotty continued working slowly and methodically, without the slightest twinge of pain in her head.

She wasn't sure what time it was when Constable Varma rushed into the office.

"Oh, toda," the constable cried, using her own, special exclamation, as she knocked into Jordan as he carried a round occasional table.

Jordan picked the table off the floor, looked at the constable in alarm, and asked Dotty, "Do you normally have police raids?" His face paled.

"This isn't a raid. There's only me, and I've just popped in to ask for a favour." Constable Varma smiled brightly.

"That's it. I've had enough. I'm not hanging around here anymore."

Jordan thrust the occasional table at Constable Varma and fled through the door into the antiques centre.

Marion walked into the office from the auction room asking, "Have you found out what Lot the table is?" She did a double take. "Constable, why are you holding that table? And where is Jordan?"

"The young man who was here?" The constable replied. "He just left, and in a hurry."

Marion stood with her hands on her hips. "He couldn't even manage a full day's work. That's what comes of sitting around playing computer games all day. Here, give me that."

Constable Varma handed her the table as Dotty said, "It's Lot 78, but there should be a pair of them."

"Thank you, Dotty." Marion pushed her tortoiseshell-framed spectacles up her nose and left the office.

Constable Varma sidled up to Dotty's desk. "I'm sorry. I didn't mean to scare him away."

Dotty leaned back. "I think it was just an excuse. He didn't look cut out to work here. Besides, I doubt he would have lasted long working with George."

Constable Varma shuddered. "Neither would I." She found the spare office chair and sat down opposite Dotty. "I've just been to Todd Mountebank's house in Swindon."

"Isn't that out of your patch? I thought you covered the villages east of Cirencester."

"Everything's quiet at the moment. Some neighbours complained about a disturbance of the peace on Saturday night in Poulton, but I spoke to the two women concerned and they swear they turned their music off at 9pm as they were both up early to work at a local riding stable the following morning."

The constable slid her hat onto Dotty's desk, pushing several pieces of paper onto Dotty's lap. She sighed. "Anyway, everyone else is suddenly 'busy', so I'm helping Inspector Evans. That's to say, I running errands for him."

"So, why have you come here?"

Constable Varma leaned forward and lowered her voice. "During my search of the victim's house, I discovered a cupboard full of boxes.

Constable Evans wants someone from Akemans to itemise what's in them, in case there's anything of value."

"Everyone's busy preparing for next week's auction and we're also compiling an inventory and valuation of paintings and valuables for the army. But let me speak to Marion and Gilly."

Dotty found the two women next door in the main auction room. "Careful," cried Marion as Gilly moved a chair and knocked it against an oak dining table.

Dotty moved from one foot to another.

Marion glanced round at her with a flash of irritation in her eyes. "Yes?"

"Inspector Evans wants someone to visit the Cirencester victim's house to identify some objects they've discovered."

"Does he now?" scowled Marion. "I'm still waiting for the police to pay for a valuation of stolen paintings David conducted three months ago. Besides, we're very busy."

"That's what I told Constable Varma," replied Dotty, looking down at her hands.

"Is that OK?" called Gilly.

Marion turned to her and gestured with her right arm. "A foot more that way."

She turned back to Dotty. "Look, can you go? It'll probably turn out to be a collection of junk, but take the camera and record everything properly, as David showed you."

When Dotty returned to the office, she found Sarah Roberts sitting on the office chair and Constable Varma leaning against Dotty's desk. More papers were scattered on the floor under her chair.

"So you filled out a missing person's report?" enquired Constable Varma.

"I felt a bit silly. He's a grown man, but it isn't like Philip to disappear like this. He's been so attentive and always lets me know when he's running late. I know he wouldn't have missed our theatre trip to Oxford last night without a very good reason."

"What did you watch?" asked Dotty.

"I didn't go. I was too worried. We were supposed to see The Imposter."

Constable Varma pushed herself up from Dotty's desk. "I'll follow it up, but as you said, there's not much we can do." She turned to Dotty and asked, "Is someone coming tomorrow?"

"Me," Dotty replied gloomily. She didn't fancy having her lack of expertise exposed by Inspector Evans.

"Excellent. It'll just be you and me to start with. The Inspector is concentrating on establishing exactly where Captain Ward, or Todd Mountebank, was killed."

"So he wasn't killed in Cirencester?"

"I think he was, but the Inspector isn't sure if his body was moved or not."

"How was he killed?" asked Dotty.

Constable Varma shuffled her feet. "We haven't released that information to the public."

"But I'm not public. I'm a consultant," replied Dotty quickly.

The constable looked from the door to the antiques centre, to the open one leading into the auction room and whispered, "He was stabbed to death."

The colour drained from Sarah Roberts' face.

CHAPTER FOURTEEN

On Wednesday evening, Dotty led Sarah Roberts through the locals' bar and into the larger front room of The Axeman pub, in Coln Akeman, the village nearest to Akemans Antiques. Horse brasses and farm implements decorated the exposed, soot-darkened wooden beams, and the curtains had been drawn in the front bay window.

"Thank you for suggesting a drink," said Sarah, as she shrugged off her coat. The log fire had been lit in the inglenook fireplace and the room was warm and inviting. "Let me buy them. What would you like?"

"A bitter lemon, please."

"Are you sure you don't want anything stronger?"

Dotty shook her head. "No thanks, I need all my wits about me driving home along the narrow lanes."

When they both had their drinks, and were settled at a small table close to the fire, Sarah asked, "Did Freddie's things arrive safely?"

"I think so. We've kept them in their crates and stored them in the secure room in the antiques centre. We'll unpack and display them after the weekend, ready for the viewing on Tuesday evening."

"Word must have got out as collectors have started calling me."

"I didn't say anything," Dotty stuttered.

"I'm sure you didn't. I expect it was Philip, drumming up interest, and the prices."

Dotty looked down at her drink and asked, "Do you really think something has happened to him?"

"Do you mean, 'has he got bored and left me?'"

Dotty's cheeks flushed.

Sarah continued, "I know that's what everyone is thinking. He's had enough of his rich widow, taken what he can and moved on. But I'm sure that's not true."

Dotty locked eyes with Sarah's and they were clear, blue and dry.

"I wasn't drawn to him that way. Sure, he's relatively good-looking and keeps himself in shape, but it's what we do, the fun we have together, that's the real attraction. I don't even think he's a real count, but I'm not bothered either way."

"Not a count. Why do you think that?"

"That stupid accent he puts on for strangers and in public. It soon slips when we are on our own. And he confused Budapest and Bucharest the other week. Budapest is the capital of Hungary, not Romania. Anyway, it doesn't matter. He's changed my whole outlook on life." Sarah stared into the fire.

Dotty sniffed the sooty air and waited for her to continue.

"I told you I was Freddie's secretary, although he liked to call me his personal assistant. He was older than me and everyone thought him the eternal bachelor. He wasn't the domestic type and spent all his time at the office or out entertaining clients. That's why I think he married me, because I could help with his business. But after he died, I was bored. I was so used to him scheduling our lives with work-related activities, and suddenly there were none. I was called in to help prepare the business for sale and now that's completed, I'm free to do what I want. But what is that?"

"Do you want to go back to work?"

Sarah picked at a fingernail. "Not really. I've been working all my life, and I don't need the money. The company sold for a high price and as Freddie was the major stakeholder, I'm a rich woman. I'm only auctioning his collection of paintings and antiques, as I'm worried about keeping them safe. It's easier to sell them."

Dotty sipped her drink before asking, "So, what next?"

"I want adventure. To travel to new places, and experience all that life and the world has to offer. That's what Philip and I have agreed to do."

Sarah's eyes began to water. "Maybe he has left me. Maybe he didn't want to be tied to a boring old widow when he could have his pick of younger women."

Dotty placed her hand on Sarah's arm. "I'm sure that's not the case."

"Well, I'll kill him for putting me through this when he does turn up."

CHAPTER FIFTEEN

On Thursday morning, Dotty arrived at Akemans Antiques as usual and began preparing for her visit to Todd Mountebank's house, the dead man Dotty knew as Captain Ward.

"You can take this tablet," declared Marion Rook as she handed it to Dotty. "David has the camera at the army barracks, so use the tablet's built in one. Are you leaving now?"

"Constable Varma's picking me up."

"And what about the Chipping Norton collection? Have you inputted everything for the catalogue?"

"I finished that yesterday, apart from the emerald brooch and a first edition of Charles Darwin's *The Origin of Species*. David hasn't provided a value for them yet."

"OK. I'll call him. George also needs to value some items, although if we run out of time, I'll leave them blank or put 'under £100'. At least people bid when they think something is good value."

"Is Jordan coming back today to help move furniture?"

"No, and his mother was very upset as he called her an interfering old …, I'm not repeating what, and told her to stay out of his life. If it were me, I'd tell him to stay out of my house."

"Hiya," called Constable Varma as she walked into the office. She didn't remove her hat, but looked at Dotty and asked, "Are you ready?"

Dotty placed the office tablet in a basket, alongside a flask of hot water, cups, tea bags, and a container of homemade biscuits. She also carried sandwiches for her and the constable in case the work took them over lunchtime. She slipped the strap of her bag over her shoulder, picked up the basket, and replied. "Just coming." She turned to Marion and said, "I'll see you later."

"Good luck. Just write down what you see, noting any maker's markings or signatures, and take lots of photos. We can fill in the blanks later. And Constable Varma," she called to the officer's retreating back, "we expect to be paid for this."

The constable shook her head as Dotty followed her out of the office.

Constable Varma drove carefully in her ancient police Mini Metro and in the limited space in the passenger seat, Dotty once again pulled her knees up to her stomach. She seemed destined to travel the back lanes of the Cotswolds in small cars.

They drove past the entrance to the Honda car factory, joined the main road, and queued down to a roundabout at the next exit. Ten minutes later, Constable Varma pulled into the drive of one of several identical interwar semi-detached houses, with a front bay window and a recessed porch. The garden next door was neat and tidy, and a garden gnome fished in a plastic tub.

Todd Mountebank's front yard was far less presentable. Two wheelie dustbins were on the path leading to the front door and one had either been pushed or fallen over, and cardboard boxes and empty plastic containers were spilling out of it.

The concrete yard, with cracks running across it, was filled with discarded items, included a cracked plastic bucket, a bent bicycle tyre and an overturned supermarket shopping trolley.

"It isn't much tidier inside," commented Constable Varma as she inserted a key into the lock and opened the front door. She stooped down to collect the day's post, which lay on the doormat and placed in on a side table. "I'll take it back to the station with me."

As Dotty followed the constable towards the stairs, she glanced through an open doorway. A small television was perched on a pine coffee table and the two-seater sofa was upholstered in a dark, floral fabric. The house smelt of damp and cooking fat. Dotty wrinkled her nose.

She was surprised when they entered a bright, clean bedroom with a striped duvet neatly pulled over a double divan bed. Constable Varma opened the doors of a fitted wardrobe, which extended across the far wall of the bedroom, and said, "There are a few shirts and jackets hanging here, but most of the wardrobe is filled with boxes."

Dotty joined her and examined the neat stack of plastic storage boxes. On the shelves were collections of smaller boxes, and everything was labelled.

Dotty pointed to a sticker on the end of a shelf and asked, "What do you think that means?"

"It's some kind of code. We haven't worked it out yet, although the numbers could be dates." Constable Varma wandered around the room. She picked up a silver photo frame from the top of a chest of drawers. "The victim and his two children." As she replaced it, she knocked off a hairbrush and box of tissues. She bent down to pick them up.

Four plastic crates were stacked on top of each other and each had a sticker with BD, and either a number nine or ten beneath. "Can I look inside these?" asked Dotty.

Constable Varma looked up. "Photograph the boxes in situ first, and then remove them one at a time."

Dotty took several photographs before removing the first box. Her pulse raced from excitement, but also trepidation. Holding her breath, she lifted the lid off the first box.

Her shoulders sagged with disappointment. From the box she removed a stack of linen napkins, tied together with brown string, and two stained linen tablecloths. Beneath them was a blue and white porcelain soup serving set. She carefully lifted the round tureen out of the box and placed it on the bed, followed by the serving dish and an attractive porcelain serving ladle with a curved handle.

"My Mum would like that, for serving curry," commented Constable Varma as she fiddled with the silver photo frame.

"I think curry would stain the pattern. It's very pretty and could be worth something, although I'm no expert." The box also contained four oval serving platters, which Dotty placed on the bed as Constable Varma plopped down, still fiddling with the silver photo frame.

"Don't do that," Dotty cried as the round soup tureen toppled over and rolled towards the end of the bed. Dotty grabbed it as Constable Varma jumped up and dropped the photo frame.

The constable's radio crackled. Still blushing, she spluttered, "I'll take this outside," and she dashed out of the room.

Dotty took photographs of all the items, wrote a short description of each, and returned them to their box. The next container also contained linen, this time embroidered tablecloths, as well as a case of silver fish knives and forks, a cake knife, and a bone-handled carving knife and matching fork.

Dotty continued her work and as she returned items to the fourth box, Constable Varma reappeared carrying two cups. She placed them on the chest of drawers and, looking sheepish, said, "I made tea. I hope it's OK, but I used the things in your basket."

Dotty smiled. "Thank you." She turned to the boxes. "I've finished with these and there wasn't anything particularly exciting. Mostly linen, crockery and cutlery. Shall I start on the top shelf and work down?"

"OK," replied the constable as she picked up the photo frame she'd dropped on the floor.

The highest shelf was marked 8S, but it appeared empty.

Dotty reached up and swept her hand across the shelf. There was something. Standing on tiptoes, she used her hand to push the item to the edge of the shelf until it toppled over. She caught a black bound book before it hit the floor.

She opened it up and realised it was a journal, and an old one, as the first date was 1910. As she flicked through, the handwriting and the colour of ink changed. Feeling guilty for prying into something private, she placed the book on top of the plastic crates.

The second shelf down had a sticker with the letters SR and numbers 04-07. There was a single plastic box which she was able to reach and pull down. It wasn't as heavy as the ones she'd previously looked in and, opening it, she was disappointed by the contents. There were horse racing cards, restaurant menus and theatre programmes.

She picked up a concert programme and noted it too was from July. Closing the box, she placed it on the bed.

The next shelf down was marked 'DD 04-05'. From it, Dotty removed a slim maroon leather case with 'V.C.' stamped on the front. She placed it on the bed, took a photo, and then opened it. She gasped.

"What it is?" asked Constable Varma.

Dotty carefully picked up the open case. "Come and look."

"I don't want to break anything."

"Don't worry, I'll hold it."

The two women stared at a Maltese cross-shaped medal with a crown in the middle, surmounted by a standing lion. There was a Latin inscription underneath, which Dotty didn't understand, and a thick maroon ribbon.

"It doesn't look very valuable. It's not silver or gold, so why are you so excited?"

"I think it's a Victoria Cross, an original. But whose is it, I wonder."

"Surely not Todd Mountebank's alter ego, Captain Ward." Constable Varma returned to the chest of drawers and picked up her cup of tea.

Dotty noticed the corner of a piece of paper poking out of the lid, under the satin lining. Using a fingernail, she prised the lining away from the case and it fell forward, revealing a folded sheet. She opened it and read, "Victoria Cross Citation. Captain Maximillian Lloyd-Roberts, Duke of Ditchford."

She paused.

"I wonder who he is," mused Constable Varma.

"I know who he was," replied Dotty. "He lived at Windrush Hall, but he died recently. I think this is the medal his groundsman, Norman Climpson, said was missing. But how would Todd Mountebank have got hold of it? Do you think he visited the dying Duke masquerading as Captain Ward?"

"I don't know, but why don't we go and ask the groundsman? Have you finished in here?"

Dotty nodded.

Constable Varma grinned. "Good. The Inspector's going to be busy all day preparing for a press conference."

CHAPTER SIXTEEN

onstable Varma parked her police Mini Metro in front of Windrush Hall and exclaimed, "Wow, this place is huge. And the old Duke lived here alone?"

During the drive, Dotty had told Constable Varma everything she could remember from her previous visit. "We'll have to be careful. I doubt Norman Climpson will be too delighted by visits from the police after what happened to the old duke."

"What do you want?" called a man from the far corner of the house. He carried a rake and wore a green wax jacket and a flat tweed cap.

Dotty extracted herself from the tiny police car.

As she approached Norman Climpson, she smelt a bonfire. "Good morning, sir. I visited last week, with David Rook from Akemans Antiques, and we met at lunch after the Remembrance parade in Cirencester."

Norman leaned the rake against the side of the house and walked towards them. "Dotty, isn't it? But why are you with the police?"

"This is Constable Varma." She turned and gestured for the constable to join her. "We've been documenting the contents of the house which belonged to the man found dead in Cirencester. And we found something we think belonged to the Duke."

"Well, you better come in and bring whatever you found with you. We can use the front door. I've mended it."

They climbed the stone steps and Norman pushed open the large front door, which had been painted with a fresh coat of grey paint. He didn't remove his mud-splattered green wellies but strode across the stone floor, through the dining room and into the Duke's living quarters. The dust sheets had been removed, and Dotty ran her finger across the top of the dining table. It had recently been polished.

"You've been working hard, Mr Climpson," she said as they entered the kitchen.

"The devil makes work for idle hands," grunted Norman.

Earl Grey, the old Duke's large furry grey cat, yawned and jumped down from the armchair where it had been curled up next to the log burning fire. It sauntered towards Dotty and Constable Varma, locking eyes with Dotty. Without warning, it leapt up and landed on her shoulder where it turned awkwardly around and sat up, like a large furry grey parrot.

Norman laughed. "He's taken a liking to you. The only other person he did that to was the Duke, until he got too frail. He took to guarding the Duke's bed during his final days."

Constable Varma was inching backwards. She sneezed. "Sorry, I'm allergic to cats," she snuffled.

"Show me what you have and I'll confirm if it belonged to the Duke," suggested Norman.

Dotty and her feline companion stepped away from the table. She lifted her hand and stroked Earl Grey's soft fur. He purred contentedly.

Constable Varma placed the slim maroon case, with V.C. stamped on its front, on the kitchen table.

Norman stepped closer. He looked up at the constable and asked, in a strangled voice, "May I?"

She nodded.

Reverently, he opened the box.

He removed a Swiss Army knife from his trouser pocket, flicked open a blade, and used it to part the lining away from the lid. Removing the citation, he placed the case back on the table and opened the folded sheet.

"I can't believe it. This is the Duke's medal. But where did you find it?"

He looked from the constable to Dotty.

Constable Varma asked, "Do you know a man called Todd Mountebank?"

Norman shook his head.

Dotty was thoughtful. "What about Captain Ward? He was at the Remembrance lunch. I remember you saying he looked familiar when I pointed him out at a neighbouring table."

"The name isn't familiar, and I didn't get a close look at him. But I don't understand, we've had so few visitors this year, with the Duke being ill, and I'm sure we haven't been burgled. Besides, how would either of those men know where to find the Duke's medal?"

Dotty licked her bottom lip and thought about the dead man. She looked at Constable Varma and asked, "Do you have a photograph of Todd Mountebank?"

"I do." The constable placed a photograph of a man with two children on the table. "I took it from the photograph frame in his bedroom," she explained.

Norman picked it up, but shook his head. "No, I don't recognise this man."

"May I?" asked Dotty, stretching out her hand, but not wanting to dislodge Earl Grey or get too close to Constable Varma.

Norman handed her the photograph. "I think this was taken a few years ago. The Captain Ward I knew was older than this."

"But I thought this was a photograph of Todd someone or other."

"It is. We'll explain in a minute." Dotty turned to Constable Varma. "The inspector carried a photograph of the victim, after he died. If Norman doesn't mind, and if you also have a copy, I think it would be worthwhile showing it to him."

"By all means, but I really don't think I know this man ... or men." Norman swallowed and scratched his cheek.

Constable Varma placed a large colour image of a man's face on the table beside the first photograph.

"I can see the resemblance between the men in both photos, but nothing more," noted Norman.

Earl Grey was getting heavy. Dotty lifted him down from her

shoulder and cuddled him in front of her. "Tell me about the doctor who visited the Duke. What did he look like?"

Norman shrugged. "He was of medium height and rather nondescript, apart from his glasses. They were large and square and he sported different coloured frames each visit."

"Think of those glasses, and look down at the picture of the dead man again," Dotty instructed.

Norman looked at the photograph and rubbed his chin. "Well, well. It could be Dr Rash, but why do you say he is called Todd someone?"

"He appears to have been a man with many faces. Todd Mountebank, Captain Anthony Ward and now, potentially, Dr Rash."

"Dr Rash is a great name for a doctor. What was his first name?" Constable Varma smiled.

"Hugh," replied Norman without emotion.

"Doctor huge rash," giggled the constable.

"At least someone finds it funny." Norman pulled out a chair and sat down at the kitchen table. "I suppose he didn't do any harm. The Duke had cancer and died as the hospital predicted. Dr Rash didn't speed it up. In fact, without his visits, I'm certain the Duke would have given up and died much sooner. They spent hours together playing chess or discussing notable people from the fifties and sixties. He provided solace and entertainment during the Duke's last days," mused Norman.

"But to steal his Victoria Cross … that's unforgivable."

CHAPTER SEVENTEEN

O n Saturday morning, Dotty spotted a free parking space in the centre of Fairford, the small Cotswold town where Gilly Wimsey's Aunt Beanie lived. She slowed down and indicated to turn right, but a large black Range Rover overtook her and pulled into the space.

Dotty bit her lip and looked around. There were no other free spots and the auction catalogues she had to deliver were heavy. Sighing, she continued along the road and followed signs to a small car park at the top of the main street, next to the entrance of what looked like a large estate with grass parkland and mature trees.

She glanced at her watch. 11.45 am. She still had time to deliver the brochures before the post office closed. Rather than carry the awkward, heavy box, she removed about two-thirds of the catalogues and divided them between two heavy duty shopping bags. Armed with a bag in each hand, she headed back towards the town centre.

"Dotty," called a female voice, as she crossed the road.

She turned round as Aunt Beanie strode towards her wearing a pair of walking boots, a faded but colourful patchwork wool coat, and a bright yellow headscarf. As she walked, she struck the ground as she walked with a curved handled shepherd's crook.

"Have you got next week's auction catalogues? I'm interested to see this collection from Chipping Norton my niece has told me all about." She grabbed the bag Dotty held in her left hand and marched away. "I'll carry these for you."

Dotty jogged to keep up.

"Have you seen the collection?" asked Aunt Beanie, striding forward purposefully.

"Yes," replied Dotty, a little breathlessly.

"I understand there are some rare first edition books. I must come over and have a look, if I can find someone to sit with Cliff."

"Here we are," the older woman announced. "I'm popping into the vets down the street. Is this your last stop?"

Dotty nodded.

"Excellent. Then you'll come back with me for lunch."

"I'm ..." Dotty began.

"That's settled," announced Aunt Beanie as she strode away.

Dotty pushed open the door of the post office and stood patiently in line while the four customers in front of her were served. The shop was small and cramped. She placed the bags of brochures on the floor and slowly spun the wheel of the carousel next to her, studying a range of birthday cards.

"Can I help you?" a man called.

"Sorry. I've come from Akemans, and I've brought the brochures for next week's auction."

"Great." The man beamed. "Customers have been asking for those." He leaned forward. "I hear there are some valuable items in the sale."

"News travels fast." Dotty smiled ruefully.

"We normally display a pile over on that shelf, next to where people address envelopes. You can place the spare ones underneath it."

"Thank you," replied Dotty, as she moved across to the indicated area and pulled some brochures out of a bag.

"Can I have one of those?" a lady in the queue asked.

Dotty found herself handing brochures out to everyone in the post office. She might have to replenish the stock on Monday.

Outside, Aunt Beanie was waiting for her. She flexed her fingers in her knitted, fingerless gloves before grabbing hold of her crook. "We'll collect your car and you can drive me home."

It wasn't far to Aunt Beanie's house, and they drove across a stone bridge above the River Caln, the same river which flowed beside the antiques centre.

Inside Aunt Beanie's farmhouse, the older lady stripped off her coat and gloves and threw them on top of the old armchair. She didn't remove her boots, but strode purposefully down the corridor. Dotty followed her.

As they entered the kitchen, Aunt Beanie declared, "First, can you help me inject this piglet?"

Dotty's eyes widened. "A pig. Where?"

Aunt Beanie stooped down beside the Aga cooker and motioned to a black bundle curled up on a green blanket inside a cardboard box. "A local farmer gave her to me. The rest of the litter has died from a form of swine fever."

She stood up and tipped a bottle out of a paper bag, which she'd removed from her coat pocket. "An iron injection. She's very weak, which may be from a lack of her mother's milk, but pigs are prone to anaemia."

There was a loud squeak as Aunt Beanie injected the piglet. It jumped out of its cardboard box but stopped suddenly and stood on the flagstone floor, shaking.

Aunt Beanie picked it up and placed it back in the box. "I'm sure it's scared, but the shaking is a symptom of the disease which killed its siblings."

Aunt Beanie washed her hands as Dotty watched the little creature curl up once again in its box.

"What is she called?" Dotty asked.

"Piglet."

"That's not very imaginative."

"I don't have time for imagination. Feel free to give her a name. What's that Cliff?"

Aunt Beanie wiped her hands on a tea towel as she wandered over to an armchair positioned before a large window in the conservatory section of the kitchen.

Dotty noticed an arm lying on the armrest, which must belong to Gilly's Uncle Cliff.

"Lunch, yes I'm preparing that now. Carrot and ginger soup and a slice of quiche."

Aunt Beanie returned to Dotty and asked, "Can you go into the pantry next door and fetch the large pan with orange soup in it?"

Dotty found the soup and, as it warmed on a hot plate on the Aga, she made a salad from ingredients she found in the fridge.

Aunt Beanie assisted her husband to another chair and turned on a small television positioned on top of a bookcase. She turned the sound down and said, "I hope you don't mind, but it keeps Cliff calm and occupied."

They settled down at the kitchen table with steaming bowls of soup, slices of quiche warmed in the bottom of the Aga, and Dotty's salad.

"Delicious," Dotty said appreciatively after her first spoonful of soup.

"Just what we all need at the moment to fight off coughs and cold. Carrots are full of vitamin C and I swear by ginger in the winter," remarked Aunt Beanie.

"Reverend Simms," shouted the old man, pointing at the television.

"Where?" exclaimed Aunt Beanie.

The old man continued to gesticulate towards the television screen with his spoon.

Dotty read the location on the screen. Cirencester.

"No, dear," shouted Aunt Beanie. "That's the man who was murdered on Sunday."

Film footage played and Dotty recognised herself marching beside Colonel Sutherland during the Remembrance parade. Several rows behind her, she spotted Captain Ward, and the news programme highlighted his face.

Aunt Beanie wrinkled her brow and glanced at Dotty. "Isn't that the man you waved to at lunch on Sunday?"

"Captain Ward."

Another image of a man came onto the screen. It was the photograph Constable Varma had taken from Todd Mountebank's house in Swindon.

"Why is the news calling him Todd Mountebank?"

"Reverend Simms," cried the old man again. He sounded upset.

Aunt Beanie leaned over and took his hand. "It's OK, dear."

She followed his gaze back to the screen and frowned as the old man gripped her arm with his free hand.

"What is it?" asked Dotty, her chest tightening with unease.

Aunt Beanie mused, "The dead man does resemble Reverend Simms."

CHAPTER EIGHTEEN

D otty stood beside Aunt Beanie, who was washing up the dishes from their simple, but delicious, lunch. She picked up a wet plate and rubbed it with a tea towel as she watched Uncle Cliff chuckle, presumably at something he heard through his headphones.

He had become increasingly agitated watching the news about the murder victim in Cirencester, so Aunt Beanie had settled him back in the armchair in the conservatory.

By contrast, Aunt Beanie had been quiet and thoughtful since recognising the resemblance between the dead man and her imposter vicar. She pulled the plug in the sink and water gurgled out. As she dried her hands on a grey towel, she suggested, "Let's have a cup of tea and discuss this case. I suspect you know more about it than I do."

The kettle boiled. "Is Earl Grey OK, or are you still drinking herbal teas?"

"A cup of Earl Grey would be lovely." Dotty dried the soup bowls as a citrus fragrance floated in the air.

After hanging the tea towel to dry on the rail in front of the Aga, Dotty sat down at the kitchen table opposite Aunt Beanie, who cradled her cup and began, "From the news reports, I know a man wearing a military uniform was found dead in central Cirencester on Sunday evening, propped up against the Woolmarket ram sculpture. But do you know how he was killed? Presumably the police don't think it was simply a heart attack or there wouldn't be all this TV coverage."

Dotty wrapped her hands around her own cup and disclosed, "He was stabbed. At least, that's what Constable Varma told me."

Aunt Beanie leaned back and folded her arms. "I thought you knew more than you've been letting on. But what with?"

Confused, Dotty replied, "What do you mean?"

"What was he stabbed with? A screwdriver, a flick knife, or something like this?" Aunt Beanie removed a carved piece of horn from her pocket and extracted a knife blade.

"Do you always carry that?" asked Dotty, slightly unnerved.

"Absolutely. I never know when I'll need to cut away a broken branch, or cut loose a rope. Most people around here carry something similar."

Staring at the dark patches on the knife blade, Dotty said, "I don't know what weapon was used. Constable Varma didn't give me any details."

Aunt Beanie examined her knife. "You should try to find out, but for now, let's concentrate on the victim's identity, as I'm totally confused." She closed the knife and returned it to her pocket.

Feeling more comfortable, Dotty placed her hands on the table and explained, "The police have identified the victim as Todd Mountebank, who lived in a semi-detached house in Swindon."

Aunt Beanie wrinkled her nose.

"But Colonel Sutherland identified him as Captain Anthony Ward, who we both saw at the lunch following the Remembrance parade. He must have been killed later that afternoon."

Aunt Beanie lifted her cup and commented, "So he was masquerading as an army officer. He's not the first."

Dotty bit her lip. "He might also have pretended to be a doctor."

"Really." Aunt Beanie's voice was sharp. "I hope he didn't harm anyone, or mistreat or misdiagnose them. That would be a motive for murder."

"I'm not sure about that, but we think he could have been a Dr Hugh Rash who visited the Duke of Ditchford during his dying days."

Aunt Beanie blinked, and the edges of her mouth curled up. She laughed, "At least he had a sense of humour. I wonder, Captain Anthony Ward. Yes, that's it. C A Ward, ca-ward, coward."

She tilted her head to one side. "And I hadn't thought about it before, but Reverend Seymour Simms's name could be 'say more hymns', or 'see more sins'."

Dotty paused, before asking, "Do you think Reverend Simms was another false identity? That he could also have been an altar ego of Todd Mountebank's?"

Aunt Beanie rested her arms on the table. "It's certainly possible, and I haven't seen him for over two weeks. I thought he'd stopped visiting as he heard our vicar had discovered his deception, but maybe that's not the reason, after all."

Dotty thought back to the work she'd done for the police at the victim's house.

"You don't happen to be missing a blue and white porcelain soup tureen, with a matching base and curved ladle?"

Aunt Beanie froze, and her voice sounded strangled as she replied, "I do have one. Granny Evans gave it to me. But why do you think it's missing?"

"I'll tell you in a minute. Can I see it?"

Aunt Beanie pushed back her chair. "Sure, follow me." She led Dotty back along the corridor towards the entrance, but stopped halfway down and pushed open a door into a dimly lit dining room. Turning on the overhead light, she strode across to a large, ornate mahogany sideboard and, bending down, turned a key and pulled open a cabinet door.

Dotty stood behind her as they both stared into the empty sideboard.

Aunt Beanie covered her mouth with her hand and cried, "We've been burgled!" She turned to Dotty and her hands tightened into fists. "But how did you know about the soup tureen? And that it's missing?" She gave Dotty a cold stare.

Dotty stepped back. "I didn't know anything about it but I found one, in the victim's house, on Thursday. The police asked me to catalogue all the items they'd discovered there."

"What else did you find?" Aunt Beanie's tone was sharp.

"With the soup tureen, there were some oval serving platters, silver fish knives and forks, a bone-handled carving knife …"

Aunt Beanie turned back to the sideboard and yanked open one of the drawers.

"And lots of table linen. Some of it embroidered," finished Dotty.

Aunt Beanie straightened up and, still staring at the empty drawer, she muttered, "At least you've found everything. Or I hope you have. I wonder what else has been taken?"

Dotty said, in a small voice, "I think I should go home."

"Of course, of course," replied Aunt Beanie, as if emerging from a trance. "I've kept you long enough."

Relieved, Dotty said in a stronger voice, "Thank you so much for lunch, and I hope your piglet gets better. How about calling her Agatha?"

"That's perfect." Aunt Beanie beamed and together the two women walked outside to Dotty's car.

"Is that part of your house?" Dotty asked, noticing the peeling blue paint on a door at the end of a short path, which belonged to a two-storey stone building extending from the main farmhouse.

"No, that's where our farmhand used to live with his family, before he retired and moved south to be closer to his mother-in-law. I should let it, when I find time to sort it out."

Dotty climbed into her green Skoda Fabia and drove home, thinking of the dead man and his multiple disguises.

CHAPTER NINETEEN

On Monday morning, Dotty parked in front of Akemans Antiques but she didn't immediately climb out of her car. She'd enjoyed her Sunday sleeping in unusually late, pottering about the house, and raking up leaves in the garden.

She drew in a breath. With the auction on Thursday, it was going to be a busy week. Tomorrow she would work late for the first of the viewings, when people came to inspect the items being offered for sale, and the second viewing was all day Wednesday.

She'd learned from the auction she'd helped with in September, that Tuesday evening viewings were principally a social gathering for the local gentry and well-to-do country set, who liked to see what their recently departed and hard up friends were selling.

During auction week, the front door of the auction house was unlocked, so Dotty pushed it open. Inside, Marion and David Rook had their backs to her and were leaning over the front desk.

"Good morning, Dorothy," welcomed David as he turned round to greet her. "Did you see the spread in the Sunday paper about Sarah Roberts' collection?"

He stepped away so Dotty could look down at the newspaper lying open on the reception desk.

David continued, "Of course, it will increase interest in the auction, but many of the people it'll attract won't be able to afford the high prices of this collection. I expect many genuine bidders will stay away and use a proxy agent to bid for them." He turned to his wife and said, "And I will have plenty of telephone bids to manage on Thursday."

The door opened behind Dotty.

"Hello, can I help you?" asked Marion in a snooty tone.

"I'm Thorn. I was told to turn up 'ere for some work."

Dotty turned around and found a young woman dressed all in black, with ripped trousers, gold chains and long hair dyed black.

"Thorn," repeated Marion. "We were expecting you, but I thought you were …"

"A man?"

Unabashed, Marian studied Thorn. "Quite, but you look young, fit and strong."

"Dorothy," David said, and she turned towards him.

"I have to help Marion and George organise the Chipping Norton collection today. I told Colonel Sutherland I would finish the regimental inventory later this week, but he wasn't happy about the delay and asked if you could continue the work and catalogue the items in his office. I don't expect you to value them, but take detailed notes and photographs, like we did at Sarah Roberts' house. If there's anything I'm unsure about, I can check it later in the week. Marion, do you have the camera?"

While Marion searched for the camera, David folded up the newspaper and Thorn slouched in the doorway, picking at her fingernails. At least she wasn't on her phone.

Armed with the office camera and laptop, Dotty drove back to the army barracks.

"Good morning," greeted Colonel Sutherland as she entered his office. "Thank you for coming this morning. I have various meetings and phone calls, but please ignore me and carry on with your work. I'm particularly keen for you to finish itemising everything in here and the cupboard where the inspector found you lurking." He raised an eyebrow.

Dotty looked down at her feet.

"Any questions?" the Colonel asked as he sat down at his desk.

"Did Captain Ward document any items in here?"

The Colonel pushed the rolled-up sleeve of his camouflage shirt further up his arm. "I can't remember. If he did, I'm sure it'll be in the paperwork I gave you."

The colonel picked up the telephone and instructed, "Send the Second in Command in."

Dotty decided to leave the cupboard until later and start with the paintings. The first three, positioned between the office's long sash windows, depicted kilted soldiers in various battle scenes. Dotty took photographs, made notes, and tried not to listen to the conversation between Colonel Sutherland and the other officer as they discussed arrangements for the regiment's move to Scotland.

The next painting was a charming image of an officer, from around the time of the First World War, looking affectionately at the head of a black horse, whose reins he held. The bare trees in the background of the painting, and the hardwood frame, made the scene more poignant.

"Wonderful painting, isn't it?" called Colonel Sutherland.

Dotty realised she'd been studying it for some time.

The colonel joined her and added, "It's far from the most valuable painting in the collection, and a relatively recent purchase, but I find it charming. The artist is Tom Keating. Have you heard of him?"

Dotty remembered her first day back at Akemans and the painting George Carey-Boyd had proudly shown her, which she later discovered was a fake.

Dotty volunteered, "I believe he was a British artist, from London."

"The East End, yes, and he's best known for paintings he forged, rather than his original work."

The colonel strode across to the sideboard, above which hung the large painting of the Iraqi desert scene David Rook had been interested in on their first visit.

He pointed to two paintings next to the Iraq one and declared, "And I believe these two are also by Tom Keating." The two paintings were strikingly different. One featured a group of soldiers looking at something outside the picture as they prepared to fight, and the second was more in keeping with the historic battle scenes of the paintings which hung between the sash windows.

Colonel Sutherland looked down at the sideboard and instructed,

"Only these two trophies belong to the mess. The other items are mine, so please don't include them in your inventory."

He moved back to his desk and picked up his phone, which had begun to ring. As he conducted his conversation, Dotty photographed and made notes about the remaining paintings. She removed Captain Ward's paperwork from her bag and flicked through it. 'CO's Office.' She scanned through a list of trophies and statues and turned to the next sheet. It was headed '2IC's Office'.

Captain Ward had not completed his inventory of this office, but he had recorded some items, which Dotty checked before copying his description. Although he wasn't a professional valuer, it was clear from his notes that he was knowledgeable about Scottish military history.

Having completed her work in the colonel's office, she entered the cupboard hidden in the wood panelling behind the colonel's desk. Was it her imagination, or were the shelves emptier than when she'd hidden from Inspector Evans? And where was the box of bubble-wrapped pictures?

"Goodbye," said Colonel Sutherland, and she heard him put the phone down.

Stepping out of the cupboard, Dotty cleared her throat. "Excuse me, sir. But there was a box of paintings on the floor when I was last here. Do you know where it is?"

The colonel shook his head and said, "I think you're mistaken, but if there was a box, it didn't contain paintings. All the regimental ones are hung on the walls."

The telephone rang again. Colonel Sutherland turned round and picked it up. "Good morning, Brigadier."

Dotty returned to the cupboard. There had been a box, but she couldn't be certain it held paintings. Perhaps it had been full of framed certificates to be handed out to members of the regiment, or something like that. She shrugged her shoulders and continued with her work.

CHAPTER TWENTY

W hen Dotty returned to Akemans on Monday afternoon, she felt the tension as soon as she opened the office door.

Marion Rook slammed the phone down and announced, "I'm recording a message for the answering machine tomorrow. At least that way I can get some work done. And why do people always call and ask the same question? Our viewing times are the same every month, and it's easy enough to check them on our website."

David Rook entered the office from the auction room. He put his mobile phone in his pocket and looked from Dotty to Marion. "I think we need a private viewing tomorrow afternoon for serious buyers and agents. George and I have spent all day fielding calls."

"So have I," grumbled Marion, and she tapped her fingers on the desk.

"Not there, there, you imbecile," shouted George Carey-Boyd from the main auction room.

Marian rolled her eyes.

"Excuse me," said David, his face set. He returned to the auction room.

Dotty heard him placate George. "Now, now, my dear Georgina. There's no need for name-calling. I know this is a very stressful time, but Thorn is trying her best, aren't you?"

Dotty didn't hear Thorn's reply.

The phone rang. Marion picked it up and in an exasperated tone answered, "Akemans Antiques."

She sat up straight and pushed her glasses up her nose. She mouthed to Dotty, "Fetch David."

Dotty found David in the auction room and gave him Marion's message. As he returned to the office, Dotty looked around. She was amazed by the transformation of the empty, barn-like space the auction room was for most of the month, into this fascinating arrangement of tables, chairs and other furniture. It would be even better tomorrow evening, for the first viewing, with soft lighting from lamps, strategically placed flower arrangements and the full effect of the central heating.

She heard raised voices from the smaller room at the far end of the auction house, where paintings were hung, and the most valuable collectables and jewellery were displayed in glass cabinets.

"You idiot. That's worth a small fortune."

The black-headed Thorn stormed out of the room. "Do it yourself then." As she passed Dotty, she asked, "How can you work here? For that …"

But Dotty didn't hear what, as George appeared and shouted at her, "Here, come and help me."

Dotty had been impressed by the main auction room, but this smaller room was even better and glittered like an Aladdin's cave. Dotty recognised the gilded mantle clock with its chariot and horses displayed in one of the glass cabinets.

"These first editions need arranging in the bookcase I've brought from home," instructed George. "But be careful. Some are old and fragile."

David entered the room. "I've just spoken to Thorn. I know she's rather prickly, Georgina, but you cannot go round shouting at people like that. They won't put up with it. I've tried to talk her around, but she's adamant she's leaving."

"She was useless anyway. No initiative."

David sighed. "This auction has attracted huge interest and we need staff to assist us." He looked around the room and its valuable contents. "But my principal concern is security, both now and during the auction. I suggest we employ a security firm until the end of the week and, since we don't have a porter, ask Vintage Removals to help on Thursday. The rest of us will be too busy to fetch and carry, and I'd like someone to double-check receipts and match them with the correct items. We can't afford any mistakes."

George crossed her arms. "I suppose we won't find a porter before Thursday, but Vintage Removals won't be cheap, and there'll be the extra security cost."

"I'll discuss it with Sarah Roberts, and see if I can persuade her to pay for it, or at least contribute towards the cost. Is everything ready?"

Dotty placed the last book in the bookcase and stood up.

"Those paintings need hanging." George pointed to a box standing beside a glass cabinet.

Dotty removed a picture which was wrapped in strong brown paper and secured with tape.

"And I've agreed we'll hold a private, invite only viewing tomorrow afternoon," revealed David.

"What?" cried George. "Why did you do that?"

"I've just had a buyer from Sotheby's on the phone. I could hardly refuse him."

George's eyes widened. She patted her hair and announced, "And we should invite the local press."

The auction office and reception area of Akemans was packed with people on Tuesday morning. Dotty sat at the reception desk answering telephone calls, which allowed Marion time to organise the film crews and journalists.

Sarah Roberts squeezed between two television crews and appeared in front of Dotty's desk. She was wide-eyed and gulped. "When David called and suggested I speak to the press about Freddie's collection, I hadn't expected this circus."

David joined them. "I'm afraid that's what happens when Georgina gets an idea into her head. And it doesn't help that all the journalists staying in Cirencester are restless, as the police aren't releasing any more information about that murdered man." He looked down at Dotty, and asked, "Everything OK?"

Dotty rubbed her forehead. "I feel the beginning of a headache, but hopefully it'll subside when your press conference starts."

"Point taken." David turned to Sarah. "Would you like to come with me and see the collection? And we can run through several questions I anticipate the journalists may ask."

As they left, the phone rang and Dotty picked it up.

"No, the viewing this afternoon is invitation only. We are open to the public at four."

As the man began to shout expletives about being treated with respect, she replaced the receiver. Her head started to throb.

"Welcome, everyone," beamed George Carey-Boyd as she entered from the auction room. She was smartly dressed in a grey trouser suit and she'd secured her glossy blond hair with a large black clip. "I'm delighted you could join us. Come through."

As the throng departed, Dotty walked to the back of the office and switched on the kettle. Perhaps some soothing camomile tea would help her ease her headache.

The door opened, and Dotty looked round.

"Am I just in time for tea?" asked Aunt Beanie as she removed her faded patchwork wool coat and hung it up on the coat stand, in the corner of the office.

Dotty's mouth fell open.

"I thought I'd dress up today." Aunt Beanie swirled around laughing. She wore a rainbow coloured tunic over black leggings and the walking boots she'd worn on Saturday. Today, her headscarf was bright purple, and it was tied with a large bow, at a jaunty angle, on top of her head.

"I don't suppose you have any Earl Grey tea?"

Dotty pulled a box down from the cupboard above her and was about to shake her head when a wave of pain swept through it. Wincing, she replied, "Just Yorkshire tea, or I'm having camomile."

"Camomile will do just fine." Aunt Beanie rubbed her knees.

"Are you all right?"

"My knees always ache before a storm, because of the low

pressure." Aunt Beanie took the cup Dotty handed her and sipped appreciatively, before asking, "Why is the car park so full?"

Dotty returned to her desk but didn't sit down. She massaged her brow before replying, in a tired voice, "George is holding a press conference about Thursday's auction."

"Cowslips," muttered Aunt Beanie. "I popped in to have a look around. Mrs Todd agreed to keep an eye on Cliff for a couple of hours."

The phone rang again and, as Dotty picked it up, Aunt Beanie sat down in the office chair.

"That's right, we open our doors at four o'clock." Wearily, Dotty replaced the receiver and looked up as the front door opened and the brown suited, barrel chested Inspector Evans of Cirencester police stepped into the office. That was all she needed.

CHAPTER TWENTY-ONE

Constable Varma followed the inspector in and closed the door behind her.

"Is Mrs Sarah Roberts here?" the inspector asked, in his deep melodic voice. "I'd like to speak to her about a missing person report she filed."

"Why is an inspector concerned about a missing person?" Aunt Beanie asked, leaning back in her chair.

The inspector narrowed his eyes at her.

Constable Varma sidestepped past the inspector and whispered to Dotty, "It's to do with that count she was telling us about last week."

Aunt Beanie leaned forward. "What count?"

"Count Philip D'Enliss."

"Constable," growled Inspector Evans. "That information is not for public knowledge."

Aunt Beanie guffawed, and they all turned to stare at her.

"It's somewhat contrived, and not as good as the Doctor but I still declare he had a sense of humour."

Inspector Evans' cheeks flushed. "Who did?"

"Your dead man, Todd what's-his-name."

The inspector strode across and towered over the seated Aunt Beanie.

"What do you know of our victim?"

"That he liked to have fun with words."

At that moment Marion Rook appeared, escorting Sarah Roberts.

Aunt Beanie continued. "Count Philip D'Enliss. Pe-d-eniless. Penniless."

Sarah Roberts took a step back. "Philip. Have you found Philip?"

Inspector Evans stared at Aunt Beanie, who looked back with a guileless expression. He grunted, "That's a stretch," before turning to Sarah Roberts and replying, "In a manner of speaking, we have."

Dotty took a deep breath, stood up, and approached Sarah Roberts. "Come and sit on the sofa. I think the inspector has something to tell you."

Sarah's hand shot to her mouth, but she allowed Dotty to lead her to the grey sofa in the corner of the reception area. "Something's happened to him, hasn't it?"

Constable Varma sat down opposite Dotty and Sarah Roberts and placed her police hat on the table. She said, "In your report, you stated that Count Philip hadn't turned up for a trip to the theatre on Tuesday night, but when did you last see him?"

Sarah Roberts was pale and her hands shook. "On Friday morning, when we left my house in Chipping Norton. I presume he was heading home, and I was attending a weekend wellness retreat at Ravenswick Hall."

Constable Varma asked gently, "And did you see or hear from him again after that?"

Sarah Roberts bit her lip and shook her head.

Inspector Evans called across in his baritone voice, "His house. Did you visit it?"

"No. I'm not sure exactly where it is. He was rather vague."

"I'm sure he was," replied the inspector, staring at the ceiling.

The phone rang.

Marion, who was standing in front of the reception desk, said, "I need to take this. Can you all move over to the corner?"

Inspector Evans strode across and rested his hands on the back of a grey tub chair.

Aunt Beanie remained sitting in her chair as she wheeled it across the reception area and stopped by a temporary plastic table, which had been set up in readiness for the auction, between the reception desk and door into the auction room.

Sarah Roberts looked across at her and asked, "What did you say about Philip's name?"

"That, at a stretch, it could be construed as 'penniless'. What do you think about that?" asked Aunt Beanie pragmatically.

"If you don't mind," boomed the inspector.

"Shush," called Marion before returning to her telephone conversation.

Aunt Beanie said tartly, "If you were going to say that you're the one asking the questions, carry on. But I think we should hear what this lady thought about the man who wormed his way into her life pretending to be someone he wasn't." Aunt Beanie slapped her hands on her thighs.

Sarah Roberts looked down at her hands and toyed with her wedding ring. She looked up at Dotty and said, "I told you I didn't believe he was a real count, because of the way he lost his European accent when we were together."

She turned towards the inspector. "But he was kind and attentive and helped me see that there is more to life than work, my husband's work. He suggested I sell the business, and my husband's collection of antiques, and travel the world with him."

"I'm sure he did," grunted the inspector.

Dotty said, in a quiet voice, "You were very generous and offered to pay for me to join you on your wellness weekend. Did you always pay for the things you and Philip did together?"

Sarah smiled at her. "I was happy to. I've more than enough money. Besides, he told me he was having trouble transferring his funds from Eastern Europe."

Dotty looked up at the inspector who made a strangled sound in his throat.

Sarah Roberts asked, "So, have you found him?" Her voice rose. "Is that what you came here to tell me?"

Inspector Evans and Constable Varma exchanged uncertain glances.

Dotty cleared her throat. "I think what the inspector is struggling to tell you is that the man you knew as Philip has died. In fact, he's the man who was murdered in Cirencester on Sunday."

Sarah Roberts blinked rapidly.

"We found a room at the dead man's house," blurted Constable Varma, "which was full of clothes and makeup. And the post I collected was addressed to several different men."

Sarah Roberts whispered, "So he wasn't a count, and he wasn't even called Philip?"

Inspector Evans cleared his throat. "His real name, as far as we can determine, was Todd Mountebank. And we're trying to ascertain how many aliases he had."

"And he was a crook and thief," retorted Aunt Beanie.

Dotty rubbed her forehead as she glanced across at the older woman. "I think it's time to tell the inspector about the Reverend Simms."

"Oh, yes," gushed Constable Varma. "I found a priest's outfit."

Aunt Beanie crossed her arms. "All I'm saying for the moment is that we've been visited by a Reverend Seymour Simms and, according to Dotty, he's been stealing our crockery and cutlery."

"I'm not being funny, but I'm supposed to be the police officer and I don't know anything about stolen kitchen items. So why do you claim to, young lady?"

Everyone turned to Dotty.

She gulped and felt the heat rise in her face. Her head pounded. "I'm the Akemans representative who's been cataloguing the stolen items at the deceased's house. There were several boxes of linen, crockery and cutlery and after Aunt Beanie thought she recognised the dead man on TV, we checked her dining room and found many items were missing. The ones I'd seen in Todd Mountebank's house."

Constable Varma removed a notebook and flipped through it. "The boxes marked BD 09-10."

"BD, that's me, Bernadette Devereux."

Inspector Evans considered her, and a smile twitched at the corner of her mouth.

"I know, Inspector, it's rather a grand name. That's why most people call me Aunt Beanie, or plain Beanie. But my husband's family, the Devereux, can be traced back to William the Conqueror."

"An old family then," remarked the inspector.

"Not for some of the locals. They still considered us incomers." Aunt Beanie sat stiffly.

"And there's the medal you found," prompted Constable Varma.

With her hand pressed to her forehead, Dotty confirmed, "Yes, we checked with Norman Climpson ..."

Aunt Beanie brightened and interjected, "The nice man we sat with at the Remembrance lunch?"

"That's right." Dotty smiled weakly. "He confirmed we did find the old Duke's Victoria Cross at Todd Mountebank's house, but the only person who'd spent any time at Windrush Hall, apart from Norman, was Dr Hugh Rash."

Aunt Beanie grinned. "That's actually the best name of all. Dr Hugh Rash. Huge Rash."

"Oh, isn't it?" cried Constable Varma as she knocked into the coffee table. A pile of magazines fell to the floor.

"Oh, toda," exclaimed the constable.

"Don't worry," said Dotty, placing the magazines back on the table.

"And the army officer, Constable. Did you get his name?"

"Captain Anthony Ward," replied Constable Varma enthusiastically. "Todd Mountebank must have spent a fortune on military uniform. But what's so funny about that name?"

"C A Ward. Coward," stated Aunt Beanie dryly.

"Oh, yeah." The constable laughed again.

"Excuse me, ladies. This is hardly a laughing matter." The inspector tapped his foot on the floor.

"Sorry," apologised Constable Varma, bowing her head but still smiling.

"Returning to the case," stated the inspector. "Our dead man, Todd Mountebank was masquerading as army Captain Anthony Ward, he was. And we think he could have been the impoverished Count Philip D'Enliss, and also a crooked priest, whose name was Reverend Simms?"

Aunt Beanie nodded.

"And possibly as Dr Rash," added the inspector sourly.

Dotty needed some air, but she said, in a fragile voice, "Norman

Climpson thought the dead man resembled the doctor, but he hadn't seen him since the Duke's death."

"Hadn't he?" mused Inspector Evans.

CHAPTER TWENTY-TWO

D otty was relieved when the door to the main auction room opened and a crowd of journalists spilled into the reception and office area.

An eagle-eyed journalist looked from Inspector Evans to Sarah Roberts and called, "Inspector, what has Mrs Roberts got to do with the murdered man in Cirencester?"

Inspector Evans pushed himself away from the grey tub chair he was leaning on and lurched towards the office door.

"Constable," he summoned in his deep baritone voice.

Constable Varma jumped up. She grabbed her hat, but as she turned, she once again knocked over the pile of magazines. "Sorry," she called as she raced after the inspector, ramming her hat on her head.

The pack of journalists turned on Sarah Roberts.

"Why was the inspector interviewing you?"

"What do you know about the dead man?"

"Were you in a relationship with him?"

Aunt Beanie propelled herself and the office chair into the centre of the reception area, and called, "What is your opinion of the auction? Is it worth a look for an old country bumpkin like myself?"

"Only if you've thousands of pounds stuffed under your mattress," replied a male voice. The pack laughed.

Dotty jumped to her feet, grabbed Sarah Roberts and fled towards the front door.

"I fancied Charles Darwin's *The Origin of Species*," continued Aunt Beanie.

"It's too late for you, love," another voice retorted.

Dotty heard more laughter as she closed the door behind her.

Constable Varma was leaning forward and talking to someone through an open car window. She looked up when Dotty and Sarah appeared, nodded to the occupant of the car and scurried towards the entrance of the antiques centre, motioning for Dotty and Sarah to join her.

As they reached the large oak door Constable Varma explained, "Mrs Roberts, the inspector wants me to check a few things with you, and Gilly Wimsey said we can use her office, which is good as it's upstairs, away from the crowd of journalists."

Dotty closed her eyes and massaged the sides of her head.

"Are you all right?" Sarah Roberts asked, a note of anxiety in her voice.

"I hope so, but you'd better go with Constable Varma. I doubt Aunt Beanie will hold the journalists off for long."

Constable Varma pushed open the large door to the antiques centre and asked, "Can you bring Aunt Beanie up when she appears?"

Dotty leaned against the stone wall of the antiques centre. The fresh, chill air felt revitalising, and she inhaled deep lungfuls.

She heard voices and shouts as members of the press emerged from the auction house.

"There she is," called a deep male voice.

"That's not Sarah Roberts," a female voice responded.

They spilled out into the car park.

Several minutes later, Dotty heard a scrunch of gravel and looked up as Aunt Beanie approached, her eyes sparkling. "That was fun. Did Sarah Roberts get away?"

"Only as far as the car park. Constable Varma's taken her up to Gilly's office for further questioning, and she wants you to join them."

Aunt Beanie stepped back and considered Dotty. "You looked

drained. Why don't you go to Gilly's office as well, and I'll bring you a cup of camomile tea."

Wearily, Dotty pushed herself away from the wall and muttered, "Thanks, but I've got work to do."

"Not for the next half an hour. I'll tell Marion that the police want to question all of us, which is close enough to the truth."

Dotty opened the door and wearily climbed the metal staircase to Gilly Wimsey's first floor office. She and Gilly hadn't finished sorting out the collection of boxes which had littered the floor, but at least they were pushed into one corner and the rest of the room was relatively tidy. She slumped down on a chair just inside the office door and lowered her head to her chest.

"We heard the press leave," Constable Varma explained. "Is Aunt Beanie joining us?"

"Yes," responded Dotty dully. She held her head between her hands and started to massage it.

Climbing the stairs had renewed the thumping in her head. She was aware of Constable Varma and Sarah Roberts speaking, but the words were incoherent. A warm, sweet tobacco smell drifted through the air and she looked up as Aunt Beanie held out a cup of camomile tea. The older lady's face was full of concern. Gratefully, Dotty took the cup and whispered, "Thank you."

She was aware of Constable Varma speaking. "Mrs Derview ..."

"Devereux. But call me Aunt Beanie. It will be much easier for all of us."

Constable Varma was sitting behind Gilly's desk and she looked uncomfortable as she cleared her throat. "Aunt Beanie, how long had Reverend Simms been visiting you, and when did you first suspect he wasn't a real priest?"

Aunt Beanie dragged the spare chair from beside Dotty across to the desk, and sat down opposite the constable, next to Sarah Roberts.

She told her story to Constable Varma and ended by telling her about the parish vicar's visit. "And I'd given him my harvest festival donation." She leaned forward. "Did you find any damson gin along with everything else he stole from me?"

"There might have been some in the kitchen, but I hardly spent any time there. It was filthy." Constable Varma wrinkled her nose and turned to Sarah Roberts. "And you're sure he didn't steal anything from you?"

Sarah shrugged. "I haven't found anything missing and look at all the valuable items he had access to."

Aunt Beanie drummed her fingers on the desk and Dotty felt as if they were inside her head. She must have made a sound as Aunt Beanie looked round sharply and said, "Sorry."

She turned back to Sarah Roberts. "The items you are selling stand a far higher chance of reaching their potential value at public auction, rather than being sold to local antique shops. Besides, any shop owner would ask questions about ownership and provenance. The items he took from me could have been sold anywhere, most probably at car boot sales."

"Oh, I love rummaging around stalls at car boot sales," enthused Constable Varma.

"But not to buy stolen items," quipped Aunt Beanie.

"Of course not," Constable Varma hung her head.

"I guess you're right about Freddie's things. Look at all the interest this sale has generated."

Dotty considered the dead man as the army officer, and as the count. The two identities she had briefly met. His face had been open and sincere, and his eyes full of amusement.

Unaware, she spoke her thoughts out loud. "I don't think he was an evil man, or that he wanted to harm any of us. Remember how long he spent sitting with Uncle Cliff and the old Duke? He talked to them, played cards and chess, and brightened up their days. And he helped Sarah experience more of life. I don't know his background, but what if he suffered a terrible tragedy, or something awful happened to him?"

She looked up to sip her tea and found the other women staring at her. Her cheeks flushed.

Constable Varma reached for her notebook and knocked over a pot of pens. Flustered, she collected them before they rolled onto the floor.

She picked up her notebook and read, "Todd Mountebank lived in London with his wife and two children. He worked in London, in some city job, but he was accused of embezzlement and sacked. His wife was having an affair with a colleague and she left him, taking their children with her. He insisted he was innocent of the charges made against him and spent a fortune on legal fees trying to clear his name."

She looked up. "Poor man, he never succeeded. And he was forced to sell the family home to pay his legal fees. His wife told a colleague of mine that she hadn't seen him for two years, even though they were still legally married."

"And his children?" asked Dotty.

The constable replied in a flat tone, "Grown up, but they hadn't seen or spoken to him recently."

"And where were his wife and children last Sunday when he was killed?" pressed Dotty.

Constable Varma consulted her notes again. "His son is abroad and his daughter was at her boyfriend's. And his wife and her partner were at a lunch, so they are all accounted for."

"Does the Inspector believe someone local killed him?" Dotty hoped she wasn't pushing Constable Varma too far.

The constable screwed up her mouth. "I've no idea what he thinks, but he was in an ugly mood when he left. To tell you the truth, I'd rather be here, questioning all of you, than back at the station with him. But I hope he does make some progress soon, or he'll be unbearable."

Dotty's mind was clearing and the throbbing in her head was receding. "Did you say you found outfits and makeup at Todd's house?"

Constable Varma brightened. "His spare room was like a theatre dressing room. You know those mirrors with the three lights above? There was one of those, and he had several full-length mirrors. We found three sets of costumes. An army officer, a vicar and a policeman."

"Policeman," cried Aunt Beanie. "What do you think he did with that?"

"I've no idea, and I daren't tell the inspector, not yet." The constable grimaced.

"So there wasn't a costume for Philip?" asked Sarah Roberts. "Maybe there's been a mistake."

Constable Varma flattened her lips as she looked sympathetically at Sarah Roberts. "I'm sorry, but I think a plastic box labelled 'Philip' confirms he was Todd. Inside it were several pairs of round glasses, and some fake beards and moustaches. Does that sound familiar?"

Sarah looked down at her hands.

"And we found a box filled with concert programmes, race cards and that sort of thing."

"All the events we attended together." Sarah Roberts sounded wistful as she wiped her eye.

"And the doctor?" asked Dotty.

"Another box was labelled 'Hugh' and contained pairs of large square glasses, each with different brightly coloured frames."

"Which, if you remember, is how Norman Climpson described the doctor who visited the Duke," noted Dotty.

Constable Varma held Dotty's gaze.

"There can be no doubt, then," stated Sarah Roberts, in a flat tone.

"I'm afraid not." Constable Varma shook her head.

There was silence.

Dotty asked, "Have you found anyone who knew the real man, Todd Mountebank?"

Constable Varma shook her head again. "Not outside London, and even there nobody has seen him for at least two years."

"What about his neighbours?" scoffed Aunt Beanie.

Constable Varma's shoulders slumped. "They were always changing, except for the old man who lived next door. He mentioned lots of distinguished visitors, but I think he was confused by Todd's different disguises."

"So we're left with a vicar, an army officer, a doctor and a count," reasoned Dotty.

"And a policeman. Don't forget him," remonstrated Aunt Beanie.

"OK, and a policeman."

"I know the suspects the inspector will focus on," revealed the constable, leaning back.

"Who?" demanded Aunt Beanie.

"You." Constable Varma smiled apologetically at Sarah Roberts.

"I had no reason to harm Philip. Quite the opposite. We were planning a wonderful and exciting new life together."

The constable gave Sarah a sympathetic look and turned to Aunt Beanie. "Then he'll move on to you and your husband."

"Cliff. He doesn't know what day it is. Besides, he has no idea Reverend Simms was a phoney, and I'd like to keep it that way. He'll only get agitated if you ask him questions, and he's more likely to tell you what happened twenty years ago, than last week."

Constable Varma leaned forward. "If I take your statement, it might delay the inspector, but I'm not sure for how long."

Aunt Beanie puffed out her chest. "I can deal with that Welsh tyrant. Besides, I used to be friends with his mum, when we both attended the Cirencester Horticulture Society. He's a mummy's boy at heart."

"I knew it," exclaimed Constable Varma. "He often receives calls and disappears to take them. And when he returns, he looks very sheepish. You must tell me all about her sometime."

Dotty was just managing to hold her headache at bay, and she knew Marion needed her back in the office. "I need to go," she said, "and I think I know who else the inspector will consider suspects."

Constable Varma leaned forward. "Norman Climpson, because of the Duke and his missing medal. And someone in the military who was associated with Captain Anthony Ward."

Dotty stood up and said, "I met him with the commanding officer, and it was under his direction that Todd Mountebank, as Captain Ward, was collating the regimental inventory."

"Exactly, and he was in Cirencester on Sunday," confirmed Constable Varma. She clapped her hands together as she turned back to Aunt Beanie. "And you were at the Remembrance lunch, too."

Aunt Beanie's face was pinched. "So what, I was helping out on the church stall in the Corn Hall. Besides, both Dotty and Norman were with me."

"So Norman Climpson is another of the inspector's potential suspects who was in Cirencester on the fateful day." Constable Varma turned to Sarah Roberts and remarked, "At least you weren't."

Sarah Roberts swallowed. "No, I was at a wellness retreat."

Dotty narrowed her eyes, which hurt her head. She was certain Sarah had waved at her, during the march and from the restaurant in the Corn Hall Arcade. So why had she just lied?

CHAPTER TWENTY-THREE

D otty left Constable Varma and Aunt Beanie in Gilly Wimsey's first floor office in the antiques centre. She walked down the stairs with Sarah Roberts and asked, "Are you staying for the VIP viewing this afternoon?"

"Georgina Carey-Boyd has asked me to, but I'm not sure I have the strength after all that's happened this morning. I might just drive home and curl up on the sofa with a good book."

"Ah, there you are, Dotty," declared Marion Rook. "Excellent. Mrs Roberts, David would like to take you to lunch at The Axeman, to recharge your batteries before this afternoon's invitation only viewing."

Sarah turned to Dotty as they stepped off the bottom step. "I guess that book will have to wait until this evening." She smiled weakly.

Dotty touched Sarah's arm. "It'll be lovely and snug in the pub with the log fire." She didn't add that she hoped there'd be no journalists there.

Back in the auction house office, Marion announced, "We have lots of work to catch up on. Can you start by arranging catalogues and forms on the plastic table for this afternoon's viewings?"

This was the second auction Dotty had been involved with at

Akemans, although the first in September seemed a long time ago. She hoped she'd remember exactly what she needed to do.

Marion continued, "I've put everything on the spare desk, but you'll have to sort through it all, as I haven't had time."

Dotty worked slowly and methodically, arranging the different auction forms into piles on the spare desk. She found a linen table cloth folded up on the plastic table, so she covered the table with it and arranged two stacks of brochures at one end, pushing the box containing the spare ones underneath the table.

There were forms for registering to bid and, for those who could not attend the auction in person, proxy bidding forms. Dotty would take the information from these and enter it into the auction system so that, during the auction, the bids would be recognised along with those from the internet and from people physically bidding in the auction room.

Constable Varma appeared from the antiques centre and rubbed her hand over her face. "I'm tired and famished. I wish I'd brought some lunch with me." She moved restlessly from one foot to another.

Dotty felt a flutter of guilt and suggested, "You can share mine, although half of them have ham in, but are you OK with egg mayonnaise and cress?"

Constable Varma grinned. "Absolutely. I love your sandwiches."

Dotty made them both hot drinks, and they sat down on the grey tub chairs and sofa at the reclaimed-elm coffee table, in the corner of the reception area. Dotty opened a foil packet and slid it across the table to Constable Varma. "The egg ones are closest to you."

They both bit into their sandwiches, and Dotty leaned back against the sofa and closed her eyes.

Despite her headache, the morning had been interesting, and she was fascinated by the life, and death, of Todd Mountebank. He had lost everything and had been forced to move out of his family home in London. He'd ended up in Swindon and reinvented himself in several different guises. She'd read about introvert actors whose whole demeanour changed when they took on a new role. Perhaps Todd had been like that. He'd certainly been charming, almost playful, as both Captain Ward and Count Philip.

Constable Varma began, "Mrs Dev ... Aunt Beanie left. She told me to say she'll be back when she can get someone to mind her husband again."

"Constable ..." began Dotty.

"Please, I've told you before. When we're together, call me Keya, and we really need to organise that cinema trip we promised ourselves before you were injured."

Dotty shuddered. "I'm not sure I can cope with the loud music yet, but there might be some interesting plays in Cheltenham or Oxford."

"Or the pantomime," squealed Keya. "I haven't been to one of those for years. Promise me we can watch a pantomime."

Dotty laughed at the childlike enthusiasm of her friend. She couldn't remember when she'd last seen a pantomime either. It wasn't something Al had agreed with. "There might be a local one in Cirencester. If I remember, I'll ask Gilly, as she probably takes her children."

There was silence again. Dotty thought back to Sarah Roberts' denial of being in Cirencester on Remembrance Sunday.

She finished her sandwich and returned to the office area, looking for a company tablet, which she found in the top drawer of the spare desk. Returning to Constable Varma, she searched on the internet for the Cirencester Remembrance parade. Scrolling through footage from previous years, she came to a clip from this year and pressed play.

The sound of bagpipes filled the room. "What are you watching?" asked Keya.

"The Remembrance parade. Come and have a look."

Dotty positioned the tablet on the coffee table and Keya grabbed a second sandwich before joining Dotty on the sofa.

Dotty pointed at the screen. "Those are the pipes and drums, and there's me, marching with Colonel Sutherland, the commanding officer. The news footage I saw showed Todd Mountebank, as Captain Ward, taking part in the parade as well. Look, that's him."

"So it is," cried Keya. "Everyone looks so smart."

The footage finished. "That was from the beginning of the parade. I want to see if there's any from the end, when we marched across Market Place."

Dotty found another clip and pressed play. She instructed, "Look at the crowd this time, rather than those taking part in the parade." The camera kept up with the marchers and they were able to scan the faces of the crowd.

"That looks like Sarah Roberts," exclaimed Keya. "And she's waving."

"Exactly, I remember her waving at me, but look, she's seen someone else, and it's as if she's been slapped in the face."

The cameraman zoomed out and Captain Ward marched past. Sarah Roberts was staring at him open-mouthed.

As the parade halted, the footage stopped.

"I don't believe it," cried Constable Varma. "Sarah Roberts told me she spent all weekend at the wellness retreat, but I'm sure that was her watching the Remembrance parade."

"It was her. And later I saw her sitting in the glass-fronted restaurant in the arcade at the Corn Hall, with a group of women. And she must have seen Captain Ward as he would have walked through the arcade to reach the Remembrance lunch."

Constable Varma declared, "I think I need to speak to Sarah Roberts again." She bit into her egg sandwich.

CHAPTER TWENTY-FOUR

A t two o'clock, the first of the visitors arrived for the private auction viewing.

Marion whispered, "He's an important figure in London's Jewish community," as a gentleman with a long beard and a black skullcap entered the office, supported by a younger man wearing a black suit.

Marion stepped forward and greeted the new arrivals. "Mr Hoffman, I'm pleased you could come. Follow me."

Marion handed the two men auction catalogues and led them through to the main auction room.

An attractive man in his forties, with an abundance of dark hair styled in a quiff, approached Dotty's desk and said, "Good afternoon. Where can I find Frederick Roberts' collection?"

Dotty blushed before saying, in a breathless voice, "It's a private viewing. Please, can I take your name to make sure you're on my list?"

"Of course he's on your list," declared George, as she entered the reception area. "Gilmore, I'm delighted you could join us. How was your journey?"

Dotty looked down at her list. Gilmore Chapman. Gainfords of London.

David Rook and Sarah Roberts entered the office. Dotty looked beyond them to see if Constable Varma was following, but there was no sign of her. After watching the video footage, she'd gone outside to contact Inspector Evans and had not reappeared.

"How are you feeling?" Dotty asked Sarah.

"Fortified, for the moment."

David said, "I hadn't realised Sarah had such a tough time this morning with the police and journalists. I've promised her she only needs to greet a few of the guests and then she can head home to rest."

Dotty regarded Sarah with a sad smile. Until the police catch up with her.

David led Sarah through to the auction room and Dotty heard him greet someone. Other visitors arrived and Dotty politely checked them off against her list without interruption from George.

The door opened and Inspector Evans declared in his deep, melodic voice, "I'm back, I am."

Of course you are, thought Dotty, and she watched the red-faced Constable Varma scamper in after him.

"Where's our suspect? The constable saw her come in."

Dotty stood, but averted her gaze guiltily. She was the one who'd brought Sarah's deception to light, so she should be the one to find Sarah and break the news. With a tightness in her chest, she entered the auction room. She found Sarah in the end room, smiling and surrounded by eager faces.

Dotty hesitated, but David spotted her. "Yes, Dorothy?"

Dipping her chin, Dotty replied in a croaky voice, "There's someone here to see Sarah. An officer who doesn't like to be kept waiting."

David's eyes widened, and she thought he'd caught her reference to Inspector Evans.

"Ladies and gentleman, let me show you the delightful French Empire ormolu mantel clock." He led the group across to a glass cabinet, leaving Sarah standing by herself.

"It's the inspector, isn't it?" Clearly, Sarah had also grasped Dotty's reference.

"Yes."

"And he knows I lied, and I was in Cirencester on Sunday."

Dotty nodded.

"That was stupid of me. I knew you'd seen me. I even waved at you." She stepped closer to Dotty and implored, "But I assure you I had nothing to do with Philip, Todd's death. What did I have to gain from it?"

Dotty shrugged. "I don't know. That's a matter for the police."

Sarah followed Dotty back through the main auction room, where the arrangement of furniture and ornaments sparkled in the lamplight, and into the auction office.

Inspector Evans had made himself comfortable on the grey sofa, and he was holding a cup of coffee.

Constable Varma hovered behind a tub chair and apologised, "I hope it was OK to make the inspector a coffee."

"Of course," replied Dotty. She'd only known him to drink tea and wondered what his choice of drink meant, and how it would affect proceedings.

The inspector looked up at Dotty and was almost civil as he said, "Thank you."

Blushing, she returned to the reception desk. There was no sign of Marion, so when the telephone rang, she picked it up.

"Yes, we are open from four o'clock this evening for the public viewing."

As she replaced the receiver, she heard Inspector Evans say, "I don't mean to be funny, but you told the constable you weren't in Cirencester on Remembrance Sunday, but we've found footage which clearly shows you were."

Dotty kept her head down as she moved round and sat behind her desk. She glanced across at the corner of the room. Constable Varma and Sarah Roberts were both seated in the grey tub chairs opposite the inspector.

Sarah's head was bowed. "I'm sorry. I panicked. I knew if you were suspecting everyone who had been in close contact with one of the dead man's disguises, that would include me. But if I claimed to be at the hotel for the wellness weekend, rather than in Cirencester, you would leave me be."

Inspector Evans leaned forward. "If you lied about that, I wonder what else you've lied about, I do."

"Nothing, I promise you," responded Sarah in a desperate tone. "I watched the parade and then met the other ladies from the retreat for lunch. We all returned to Ravenswick Hall in the hotel's minibus, at three o'clock."

Dotty considered this as she tapped keys on her computer. She had left the Remembrance lunch around half-past two and Todd Mountebank, as Captain Ward had still been there.

"Constable, we need statements from the minibus driver and the other hotel guests," growled Inspector Evans.

He sat up but drummed his fingers on the table. "The thing is, did you recognise your Count Philip in Todd Mountebank's army officer disguise as Captain Ward? I've watched video footage and think you did."

Sarah looked quickly from the inspector to Constable Varma and back again. She fiddled with her gold earring. "There was a man in the parade who did resemble Philip, but I couldn't be certain. Philip had a neat beard and moustache and wore small, round glasses. The man in military uniform had a moustache, but a comedy one that curled up at the ends."

The inspector leaned towards Sarah Roberts. "But you went to find him, to check if you were right, did you?"

Sarah's shoulders slumped. "I tried to, but he was busy talking to other soldiers, and I didn't like to interrupt. What if I was wrong and embarrassed myself in front of all those people?"

"So you waited until he was alone and confronted him," the inspector pressed.

"No," cried Sarah, as if the inspector had punched her. "I went back to the hotel with the other ladies. I didn't want to miss the minibus."

David strode into the reception area and stopped beside Sarah's chair. Dotty watched his back as he tilted his head and asked in a concerned voice, "Sarah, are you all right."

Dotty didn't see or hear Sarah's response, but David turned towards the inspector and demanded, "What are you accusing Sarah of? Why is she so upset?"

Dotty watched the inspector, who leaned back and looked up at David. "I'm not accusing Mrs Roberts of anything. I just need to know what she was doing in Cirencester on Remembrance Sunday."

"And what were you doing?" asked David in a practical tone.

"Watching the parade and having lunch with friends."

David turned back to the inspector. "Satisfied?"

"For now," the inspector drawled.

David turned and entered the auction room. Dotty heard him call, "Marion."

A minute later, David and Marion returned.

"Marion, please can you help Mrs Roberts compose herself?" David said. "Gilmore Chapman in particular, is keen to speak with her."

David returned to the auction room as Marion escorted Sarah away. With narrowed eyes, the inspector watched them leave. He said in a deep, melodic voice, which carried clearly to Dotty's desk. "I'm not being funny, but that woman knows more than she's telling us."

CHAPTER TWENTY-FIVE

Dotty was excited, and relieved that it was Thursday, the day of the auction. The viewings on Tuesday evening and Wednesday had been crammed with visitors, most of whom David Rook doubted wanted to buy anything, but were attracted by the substantial press coverage the Chipping Norton collection had received.

As Dotty parked her car, she noted a dull light emanating from the auction house office even though there were no other cars in the car park. A blue-uniformed security guard opened the front door and bowed his head to light a cigarette.

With relief, Dotty got out of her car. She wouldn't have to open up or deactivate the burglar alarm. She glanced at her watch. It was only half past seven, but she needed to enter the pile of proxy bids which had built up the previous afternoon, and she was certain more would have been sent by email.

She collected her basket, which contained tins of biscuits, chocolate brownies and a Victoria sponge cake, for the small cafe Gilly Wimsey ran on auction day. Her mouth watered at the thought of the bacon butties Gilly served throughout the morning, as she hadn't had time for breakfast.

It was peaceful in the office as she switched on her computer and began to enter the proxy bids on the auction system. She had been correct. At least another twenty had been sent by email. She was looking at the first of these when David and Marion arrived.

"Good morning, Dorothy," said David as he hung his coat on the coat stand. "How pleasant to see a young person so dedicated to their work. Do you know if Georgina has arrived? I didn't see her car."

"Tea or coffee, anyone?" asked Marion, "before Gilly steals the office kettle for her cafe." As usual, Marion was immaculately turned out in a dark purple tartan skirt and a black polo-neck jumper. She wore a striking necklace with a gold disk and three purple stones.

"I haven't heard George," replied Dotty.

"Ah, but you will the moment she arrives. This is an important auction and Georgina will be wound up very tight," David warned.

Marion handed her husband an aromatic cup of coffee with the scent of cardamom and remarked, "It's your job to keep her calm. That's not Gilly's forte and she'll be busy making cups of tea and bacon sandwiches."

Dotty's stomach rumbled.

"And Dotty and I will have more than enough to do." She glanced at her watch. "The men from Vintage Removals are due at half-past eight, so I can show them where everything is and explain the collection procedure. Have you finished inputting the proxy bids?"

"Nearly, the only ones left are those emailed last night."

Marion nodded curtly. "Good. David, shall we check everything is set up correctly?"

The next person to arrive in the office was Gilly. She looked remarkably well turned out. Her mass of orange curls was neatly arranged, and she wore a comfortable but tasteful navy skirt and blue spotted top.

Dotty reached around for her basket. "I made a Victoria sponge again, some biscuits and some chocolate brownies."

Gilly beamed. "You are a star. I don't know how you remember, or had the time after such a busy week. I had to rush to the supermarket last night for bacon, bread and tea bags." She picked up a branded supermarket bag and Dotty's basket. "I'll make you a bacon sandwich when I start frying."

"The screen is in totally the wrong place," screamed George Carey-Boyd from the auction room.

"Here we go," remarked Gilly, raising her eyebrows. Her shoulders slumped as she walked towards the auction room.

At quarter-past eight, the first customer arrived. "I haven't had a chance to look round yet, and I want to make sure I have a good seat for the auction," explained a round-faced man as he filled in a registration form.

Dotty wrote his bidder number on a scrap of A5 paper in large black writing. "If you are successful and have the highest bid, hold this up towards the auction rostrum so they can write your number down. Catalogues are over there, on the table." She pointed at a temporary table covered with a white cloth.

Marion appeared and with raised eyebrows, announced, "People are already arriving. I'm glad we hired some extra chairs. It's all very well people sitting on the furniture which is being auctioned, but I doubt there will be enough space, especially mid-morning when the Chipping Norton collection is scheduled for sale."

"Not like that," shouted George.

"Oh dear," sighed Marion. "I'm so glad David is here today. He's the only one who can reason with George. But she's usually OK once the auction starts. She just gets so wound up beforehand. It must be the nerves."

Gilly reappeared. "Do you mind if I take the kettle?"

She collected it from the back of the office and as she passed Dotty's desk, she enquired, "Are we still starting at half-past nine? It's just there are a lot of people already demanding teas and coffees, and I'm a bit behind."

"The usual time, half-past nine," confirmed Marion.

Some people who arrived already had their bidder numbers written out on pieces of paper and others remembered them from previous auctions.

A colourful Aunt Beanie appeared in front of Dotty's desk. She had a pink headscarf and wore a pink shirt and a grey pair of trousers with black boots. "Isn't this exciting? Mrs Todd brought her knitting over and has agreed to sit with Cliff this morning, so I'm free to watch the show. And I might even bid for something. What's my number?"

Dotty consulted her computer. "Eighty nine. Would you like me to write it out for you?"

"Yes, please." Aunt Beanie looked around. "Here comes Sarah Roberts. I must say, she's very pale, and it doesn't look like she slept at all last night with those dark rings around her eyes. I thought she'd be excited about today's sale." She turned back to Dotty. "It's been in all the papers, and there was even an interview with George on the radio this morning. Toodle-doo," she said as she wandered off.

Dotty stood up and approached Sarah, who hovered in the middle of the reception area. "Are you all right?"

Sarah grasped Dotty's arm. "It's too much. This sale. Philip's disappearance. The police questions. I just want to get away, a long way away."

Dotty said sympathetically, "I'm sure you'll be able to soon."

Sarah gripped her arm tighter. "Will you come with me? How about Vienna? We could take a horse and sleigh ride in the snow and visit the Christmas market."

Dotty's pulse increased. "That sounds fantastic."

Sarah's voice was insistent. "Then let's do it. When all this dies down."

She looked around the office, and the colour drained from her face.

Dotty suggested, "Come and sit with Gilly. She'll make you a cup of tea and I think you should have something to eat, even if it's only a biscuit."

Gilly appeared, carrying a paper plate and a foil package. "Your bacon sandwich." She looked up as the door opened again. "Although I'm not sure when you'll get time to eat it."

"Excuse me," called a haughty female voice.

"Gilly, can you look after Sarah for me? She's rather overwhelmed. And make sure she eats something."

"Sorry about that," apologised Dotty to two ladies standing by the reception desk.

"I doubt we'll find a good seat now, but someone told us we have to register with you if we want to bid. I think this is the right form." She waved a piece of paper at Dotty.

Quickly, Dotty transposed the information from the form onto her computer and it produced a bidder number, which she wrote on top of the form and, in large black writing, on a scrap of A5 paper. "Here you are, number 162. If you have the winning bid, hold this up towards the auctioneer's rostrum."

The two women peeled away from Dotty's desk, and a man who looked familiar stepped forward.

"Hello, Dotty. I can see why you enjoy working here. It's very busy and exciting."

"Colonel Sutherland," exclaimed Dotty. "I didn't expect to see you here."

"As it's likely we'll have to sell some of our silverware and paintings, I thought I'd come along and see what an auction is all about. And there's a collection of military history books I might bid for."

"Then you'll need to fill in the A4 form on the table over there." Dotty pointed to the temporary table. "Just a minute, we've run out of pens."

Dotty refilled the pot of pens and showed Colonel Sutherland which form to fill in.

She returned to her desk and entered the bidder details for several more customers.

"168," she told Colonel Sutherland after she had entered his details on the computer system. She wrote it out on a scrap of A5 paper and handed it to the Colonel.

"And I hold this up for the auctioneer to see if mine is the highest bid?" enquired the colonel.

"That's right," confirmed Dotty, smiling.

Fifteen minutes later, Dotty heard George's amplified voice announce. "Ladies and gentlemen. Please take your seats. We'll begin in five minutes." At least the microphone and loudspeaker system were working.

The reception area emptied as the remaining customers entered the auction room.

Dotty sat back and breathed a sigh of relief.

The door opened again, but the man who rushed past waved his auction brochure at her, and she saw a piece of paper with his bidder number sticking out.

George announced, in her amplified voice, "Ladies and gentlemen. Welcome to this special November auction. I'm delighted to see so many of you attending, but please, can I ask you to keep quiet during the bidding and only move around between Lots. We'll begin with Lot 1, a leaded glass and bronze floor lamp in the style of Tiffany Studios."

Dotty opened the foil packet Gilly had given her and inhaled deeply. She bit into her bacon sandwich with satisfaction.

She had just finished her sandwich when the door opened and a plump couple entered. "We're not late are we?" whispered the man as George's voice, said, "£120, any advance on 120. 130 on the internet."

"We started at half-past nine, but only a few lots have been sold."

"I told you, Arthur," scolded the woman.

"Mr and Mrs Woodman. Please can you check our bidder number?" Dotty did so and wrote it out for them.

A steady trickle of customers continued to arrive.

David appeared with the first batch of green auction sheets on which Marion wrote the bids, and the winning price and bidder number. "I thought you might still be busy, so I brought you these." He handed the sheets over. "But I won't be able to bring them all. I've several telephone bids to deal with." He stopped and considered Dotty. "In fact, can you help me?"

"Me?" Dotty felt breathless. "But all those people in there."

"My dear Dorothy, they don't bite. Besides, you'll have to go in to collect the auction sheets, and you won't get a chance to notice them when you're dealing with a customer on the other end of a phone. I have two telephone bidders for one Lot so I need you to deal with one of them. The main thing is to keep your client informed of the bidding progress and ask if they would like to raise their bid, when it is their turn. If they do, you inform Marion. I know both bidders are eager to buy the French Empire ormolu mantel clock."

Dotty still felt a tightness in her chest.

"I'll return just before the Lot, but don't forget to collect the green auction sheets."

Dotty's palms felt sticky. She was happy dealing with customers from behind her desk, but to stand in front of a packed auction room was entirely different. Who knew what might happen?

CHAPTER TWENTY-SIX

Dotty was sitting in the office of Akemans auction house worrying about how she should would cope with a customer bidding by telephone.

The door opened and Norman Climpson stepped into the office. She hadn't expected him to attend the auction. He removed his flat tweed cap and grasped it in front of him. "You're the lass who visited with the policewoman, the one who found the Duke's medal?"

"Hello, Norman. How is Earl Grey?" She remembered how the Duke's cat had jumped onto her shoulder and had remained there until he became too heavy for her to carry around.

"Pining for his master. I need to find him a new home." He raised his eyebrows and looked at her questioningly.

"He's a lovely cat, so I'm sure you'll find someone to take him." Dotty's stomach felt queasy as she thought of her new task and she wished she hadn't eaten the bacon sandwich.

"Can I go in and watch?" asked Norman.

"Of course, but I'm not sure how many free seats there are."

"That's OK. I'm happy to stand or lean against a wall. And what about bidding?"

"You need to fill in a form and I give you a number. Was there anything in particular of interest?"

"A fishing set, complete with rods, flies and fishing wire."

At the mention of fishing wire, Dotty thought she was going to be sick.

"Excuse me." She rushed to the back of the office and poured herself a glass of water.

"Are you OK?" Norman looked genuinely worried.

Dotty walked back and stood beside her desk. "Sorry, I've been asked to help in the auction room and I'm not very comfortable with large crowds."

Norman placed his hand on her arm and confided, "Neither am I."

Dotty showed him how to fill in a bidder form and after she'd entered his details, she wrote his number on a piece of paper and handed it to him. "Number 268." I don't think the item you're interested in is until after the Chipping Norton collection."

"Is that what all the fuss has been about on the radio?"

"Yes, and it is amazing."

"How does the Duke's collection compare?"

Dotty considered the question. "This collection has been collated over just a few years, whereas Windrush Hall is full of items which have been gathered over centuries. There are less high value items in the hall, but David said some of the paintings are extremely rare, and there are a few he didn't even know existed."

David appeared and called "Dorothy."

She gulped and followed him into the auction house.

Halfway down the room, on the left side, Marion and George sat on a raised platform behind a wide wooden podium. They both had computers in front of them, and a large screen behind them which displayed a photograph and a brief description of the item being sold.

In front of the podium, people sat on the chairs and sofas which were being auctioned, and the white plastic seats which had been hired to accommodate the extra customers.

Dotty tried to ignore them as she made her way across to David, who stood in front of another temporary plastic table beside the raised stage. He held two mobile phones in his hand and whispered, "I'll call the client and check he still wants to take part in the auction. I will also ask him to confirm he is happy to bid up to the estimated value of £8,000. Marion told me we have proxy bids up to £8,500."

"Lot 126," announced George.

"Ours is the next Lot. I'll call your client now."

Dotty glanced back at the faces in the room. Some people studied their catalogues, and a few appeared bored, but most were excitedly watching the bidding prices, which were displayed on the large screen.

"He's ready," said David, handing her a phone. "Introduce yourself and follow my lead."

Dotty took the phone with a shaking hand. "Hello," she whispered into it.

An Arabic voice replied in excellent, but accented, English. "Good Morning. I hope you'll help me win this clock."

"I'll certainly try."

"Lot 127. A fine French Empire ormolu mantel clock. We've had lots of interest in this item, so we can open the bidding at £7,600," stated George.

Someone close to Dotty gasped.

"And we already have £7,900 on the internet. £8,000, £8,100. £8,200. £8,300. We'll let it run."

The price on the screen continued to rise and stopped at £8,600.

"What is happening?" the voice on the phone asked.

Dotty had been transfixed by the invisible internet bidding.

"Sorry," she stammered. "Bidding on the internet has raised the price to £8,600. Would you like to bid higher?"

"Yes, I'll bid £8,700."

Dotty looked up and caught Marion's eye. She whispered, "£8,700."

The figure on the screen increased.

"£8,700 on the phone," reported George.

"Your bid has been accepted," Dotty told her client.

The figure on the screen increased again.

"Another phone bidder has raised the bid price to £8,800," said Dotty.

"Bid again," said her client.

Dotty and David consulted with their telephone clients and the price increased steadily to £9,600, against Dotty's client.

"Do you want to bid again?" she asked.

The man chuckled. "I don't think I shall win this one, as I suspect I know who I am bidding against. But let us have some fun. Offer £10,000."

"Dotty, your bid," called Marion.

"Are you sure?" Dotty asked her client.

"I'm sure."

Dotty looked up at Marion and called, "£10,000."

David looked at her sharply and relayed the news to his client. "£10,300."

"Bid £10,600, but this will be my final bid," said Dotty's client.

"£10,600," called Dotty.

"£11,000," countered David.

"Thank you for your help, young lady. I've had an amusing time. Do thank David for me and tell him I look forward to seeing him in the New Year." He finished the call.

Dotty looked up at Marion and shook her head.

"The bidding stands at £11,000," announced George. "Do we have any advance on £11,000?"

There was a hush in the room.

"Sold," called George.

Dotty was shaking, but this time from the excitement. What must it be like to have over £10,000 to play with? And what would have happened if the other caller hadn't increased his bid? Would her client have honoured his?

"Well done, Dorothy. I was surprised when your client raised his bid to £10,000. Did he say anything about the person he was bidding against?"

"He told me he thought he knew who it was."

David nodded sagely. "Still, a great result for Sarah and Akemans."

Dotty looked around the room as George announced, "Lot 128. A Mount Washington Royal Flemish vase."

Marion leaned across and waved some green sheets at Dotty.

Dotty took them and, when the bidding stopped, she crossed the room to Gilly Wimsey's small cafe area.

"Tea?" asked Gilly.

"Yes, please. Have you seen Sarah Roberts recently?"

Gilly shook her head. "She stayed with me for quite a while, and I fed her your chocolate chip cookies. That seemed to perk her up, but when the bidding on her late-husband's collection started, she vanished, and I haven't seen her since."

"She might be in the reception area. I better get back and start processing these winning bids." Dotty took the cup Gilly handed her and returned to the office and reception area, but there was no sign of Sarah.

She sat down at her desk and started work on the winning bids. Half an hour later, she heard George call, "Ladies and gentlemen. That's the end of the Chipping Norton collection. If you have bought an item, please bear with us while we prepare your invoice. For now, we'll take a fifteen minute break."

Marion bustled into the office carrying a cup of coffee. She sat down at the spare desk, on which a second computer had been set up. "Let's start with invoices for people in the room. I marked those bid sheets with an Asterix."

Dotty tried to ignore the people entering and leaving the office as she worked through the winning bids.

She looked up at a woman wearing black trousers and a green padded jacket. "Can I pay for my items?"

"I'll see if we've entered the details. What is your bidder number?"

Dotty entered 47 on the system. "I've three items listed. Is that correct?"

"It is," confirmed the woman.

Dotty printed out an invoice, which the woman checked and paid for with her credit card. Dotty stamped paid on the invoice and handed it to the woman. "Vintage Removals are in charge of packing, and checking items have been paid for. They should be easy to spot, as they're wearing maroon polo shirts."

The woman left the office.

Dotty entered another Lot while a man stood patiently in front of her desk. She looked up, and he handed her his bidder number.

As she started to enter it into the computer, someone screamed.

"Who was that?" called Marion.

Dotty jumped up and ran to the entrance of the auction room.

"A body!" a man shouted.

Dotty pushed her way through the throng of people until she met Gilly and Aunt Beanie standing at the edge of the cafe area.

"What's happening?" Dotty asked.

"Someone screamed." Gilly looked perplexed.

"It sounded as if it came from the end room," added Aunt Beanie.

Dotty pushed through more people towards the far room where the Chipping Norton Collection was on display. She met David in the doorway, holding back the crowd.

"Dorothy, thank goodness. I need to call the police, and an ambulance."

"Why? What's happened?"

"It's Sarah Roberts. And there's a lot of blood."

CHAPTER TWENTY-SEVEN

Dotty sat behind the reception desk in the office at Akemans auction house with her head in her hands.

Sarah Roberts was dead. Was it her fault? She had been the one to tell the police Sarah had been in Cirencester on Remembrance Sunday, so had she let slip some other piece of information which had compromised her or put her in danger?

She felt guilty for betraying Sarah to the police, but it hadn't seemed to affect their budding friendship, as Sarah had still asked her to go with her to Vienna.

Dotty had seen something of herself in Sarah. An obedient wife who had faithfully fulfilled her duty to her husband. And she thought Sarah had recognised the same in Dotty. A widow trying to understand and explore a world without her husband and make her own way in life.

"Dotty, dear." Aunt Beanie's voice interrupted her introspection. She lifted her head and wiped her eyes. A thumping started in her head.

Aunt Beanie dragged the spare chair across from the second desk and sat beside Dotty.

"Finding a body is traumatic, particularly when it's someone you know," sympathised Aunt Beanie.

Dotty looked at her and asked, "Why would anyone want to harm Sarah? She'd lost her husband and her ... friend, and all she wanted to do was leave the Cotswolds to explore the world with Philip. Why would someone want to stop her doing that? It's not fair."

Aunt Beanie squeezed her arm. "I've seen enough of life to know it isn't fair, and so have you. But as to why someone needed to kill Sarah, I've no idea. Perhaps there's something about her, another side, or something in her past, which led to her death. I guess that's for our Welsh officer of the law to discover."

Aunt Beanie gazed around the reception area. A group of auction clients were seated in the corner on the grey sofa and chairs, murmuring to each other in low voices.

"Talking of Inspector Evans," continued Aunt Beanie. "I hope he arrives soon and doesn't keep us here all day. Mrs Todd did me a favour today, but she won't offer again if she misses her late-afternoon bingo."

There was a loud rap on the front door. Dotty stood and as she walked towards it, she removed a small bunch of keys from her pocket. David had interpreted the inspector's instructions not to allow anyone to leave the auction by locking all the doors.

She unlocked the front door, and Inspector Evans stepped through. "At least we have someone sensible working here. I approve of locking up all the suspects, I do."

The inspector was followed by an ashen faced Constable Varma and three other uniformed officers.

"Inspector." Aunt Beanie stepped in front of the burly policeman. "My sick husband is at home, and I have to return to relieve his minder. Please, ask me any questions you like so I can get back to him."

"Mrs Devereux," remarked the inspector in a flat voice. He turned to Constable Varma and ordered, "Take her statement, and then she can go. But don't tell anyone else, they'll all want the same treatment." He turned back to Aunt Beanie. "Where's this body then?"

Aunt Beanie turned and indicated towards the auction room. "In the far room, where the men from Vintage Removals are finally keeping guard."

"And you lot," the inspector addressed the group sitting in the corner, "can return to the auction room. This space is reserved for police questioning."

The group jumped to their feet and fled into the auction room.

"Why it is, is," muttered the inspector as he left the office. The three uniformed police officers followed him into the auction room.

"Is it really Sarah Roberts?" asked Constable Varma. She stood in the middle of the reception area, clutching her black and white hat.

Dotty gulped. "I'm afraid so. And it's horrid. She was lying on the floor and her front was covered in blood."

"Who found her?" The constable looked as if she was about to burst into tears.

Dotty rubbed her own eyes. "I don't know. Marion and I were in the office when we heard a scream."

"I was helping Gilly in her cafe," added Aunt Beanie, "and I also heard a scream."

"Cafe?" asked Constable Varma, her face brightening.

"That's rather a lofty name for a few tables and chairs in the corner of the auction room," Aunt Beanie explained.

Constable Varma licked her lips.

"There were plenty of cakes and sandwich fillings but the hungry crowd has eaten most of it," apologised Aunt Beanie.

The constable's shoulders slumped. "I suppose we better get on with your interview. Shall we sit over there?" She indicated towards the sofa and chairs in the corner.

Dotty pulled a stack of green auction sheets towards her and stared at them blankly. The image of Sarah's body filled her mind. She grabbed a sheet and began inputting the data.

Constable Varma asked, "Mrs Dev … when was the last time you saw Sarah Roberts?"

"In Gilly's cafe. Lots of people arrived before the auction started, so I helped out. When Gilly returned with the office kettle, she brought Sarah Roberts with her and the poor woman looked awful, as if she hadn't slept a wink. She was very pale and, as Dotty had suggested, we managed to get her to eat something, a slice of toast and some chocolate cookies, which seemed to perk her up."

There was a pause. "I think I last saw her when George called a break before her husband's collection was auctioned. I was busy serving customers and once the auction restarted, I was too interested in the bidding to notice what anyone else was doing."

Constable Varma continued writing in her notebook. Finally, she looked up and asked, "Were you with Mrs Wimsey in the cafe all morning?"

Aunt Beanie tilted her head. "No, I don't think so. I wandered around the auction a bit, inspecting the Lots."

"And did you go into the far room?"

"Yes, once, but that was earlier, before the auction started, but I couldn't see much. It was too crowded."

Inspector Evans returned to the office, followed by David Rook.

Constable Varma jumped to her feet and Auntie Beanie followed her lead, asking, "Can I go now?"

Constable Varma looked across at Inspector Evans, who raised his eyebrows. She gulped and turned to Aunt Beanie. "I'll let you know if I need anything else. Thank you."

Aunt Beanie crossed to Dotty's desk. "Trouble concentrating?"

Dotty realised she was holding the same green auction sheet that she had picked up at the start of Aunt Beanie's interview, and she was staring at the police officers.

"I need to know what happened to Sarah Roberts, and why? I think it might be my fault." She dropped her gaze to the desk.

"Don't be ridiculous. As we discussed earlier, neither of us really knew Sarah Roberts, and there could be a myriad of reasons why someone killed her. Don't go upsetting yourself. Now I must dash, before the inspector changes his mind." She left the office.

Dotty tapped her keyboard and tried to concentrate on her work.

"Mr Rook, you called the police and ambulance service. Did you find Mrs Roberts on the floor of the auction room?"

"No, but I'm not sure who did. I was standing beside the auction rostrum, discussing with another customer how well the sale of her husband's collection had gone, when I heard a woman scream. I rushed across to the end room, as best I could through the milling crowd, and there were several people in it, but they quickly vanished when I inspected the body. I thought there was a weak pulse, which is why I wanted to call the ambulance, but I was delayed as I had to block the entrance to prevent people from entering. I knew it was a crime scene. When Dorothy arrived, I asked her to check on Sarah while I called the emergency services."

Dotty stared fixedly at the computer screen, but she felt the inspector's presence as he loomed up in front of her.

"You again. One of these days, you'll land yourself in real trouble, you will."

Dotty touched the wound on the back of her head.

"What can you tell me about the body?" the inspector asked.

Dotty squeezed her hands into tight fists and relaxed them as she breathed out. She looked up at the inspector and began, "Sarah. Sarah Roberts was lying on the floor staring up at the ceiling, and her white shirt was stained with blood."

"You're an observant woman. Did you see the wound, or an object which might have caused it?"

"You mean a weapon? I didn't notice anything, but I was more concerned about Sarah. I thought I could do something to save her." Dotty's head drooped. "But I couldn't. I knew she was dead."

The inspector waited, his shadow falling across Dotty.

Dotty composed herself and once again looked up at the inspector. She held his eye contact as she asked, "How was she killed? And what reason did anyone have for hurting her?"

"You've hit the nail on the head there, you have. That's what I want to know. As for how she was killed? She was stabbed in the heart."

CHAPTER TWENTY-EIGHT

D otty spent the next few hours trying to concentrate on her work, but she failed as her attention kept being drawn to Inspector Evans as he questioned George Carey-Boyd, Gilly Wimsey and Marion Rook.

None of them had seen Sarah Roberts enter the far room, where her husband's collection was displayed, as they had been busy with the auction, or, in Gilly's case, serving customers in her small cafe.

When the inspector wandered into the auction room, George, Marion and David gathered in the office area behind Dotty's desk.

"What are we going to do?" demanded George. "We're only halfway through the auction."

"Be thankful, Georgina, that at least we have completed the sale of the Chipping Norton collection. The question now is who is the new beneficiary?" David looked glum.

"But what about everything else?" implored George.

Marion clasped her hands in front of her. "We won't finish today and I doubt the police will let us continue tomorrow, not if they consider the whole auction house a crime scene. So either we reschedule for next week, or ask for proxy bids for the remaining Lots. With the latter, we'd have to ask the owners if they're willing to accept the highest bid but I know for a fact, the receivers are more interested in when they get their money for the restaurant equipment, rather than how much it makes."

"Let's think about it," suggested David. "I need to speak to the inspector about our security guards, as we shall have to continue with their services until we can pack up the Chipping Norton collection. At least we can offset the cost against Sarah Roberts' estate."

"This is a disaster," cried George. "The second body in three months. Who's going to want to visit Akemans after this?"

"Everyone," surmised Marion, dryly.

Marion, David, and George left the office and entered the auction room, but David soon returned, accompanied by Inspector Evans.

"Inspector, we've hired a private security firm to guard the premises while Sarah Roberts' late husband's collection is on display. They will be here tonight and every night until we are allowed to pack up the items in the far room."

"I don't want nosy parkers poking around, I don't. Can you lock that room?"

"I can, but they'll still require a key."

The inspector grunted.

David turned away, but the inspector tugged his chin and said, "Were they supposed to be guarding that end room during the auction, your security guards?"

David turned back and replied, in a flat tone, "They weren't, but we employed Vintage Antiques to provide porter services, since we lost our own porter."

David paused, and the inspector looked up at the ceiling.

David continued, "And they told me they couldn't see the large screen behind the auctioneer's rostrum, so they moved away from the entrance to the end room to watch the proceedings. I can understand why, as the auction was exhilarating."

"So anyone could have entered or left that room?"

"I'm afraid so, Inspector, and I doubt anyone noticed Sarah, or her assailant, as the entire audience was gripped by the bidding."

The inspector shook his head slowly. "I've spoken to my team. A lady was murdered under the noses of several hundred people, and nobody saw a thing." He drew his lips into a thin line.

David shifted his weight from one foot to another. "If you'll excuse me, Inspector, I'm needed inside."

David left the office and Dotty finally completed her first entry into the auction system. She picked up another green sheet, but her concentration was again interrupted as Constable Varma rushed into the room and cried, "I've found some evidence."

Inspector Evans turned to her and tilted his head to one side as he replied, "You have, have you?"

"Yes, look." The constable thrust a plastic bag towards the inspector, who pinched the top and held it up. "I'm not being funny, but it's just a number written with black ink on a scrap of paper, so why are you so excited?"

"That stain is dried blood," added the constable gleefully. She paused and her smile faded. "I found it under Sarah Roberts, when the ambulance men moved her body."

Dotty listened intently. Constable Varma had found a bidder's number.

"Well, ask your friend what it means?" suggested the inspector, sounding skeptical, and he passed the bag back to the constable.

Constable Varma approached Dotty, waving the plastic bag.

Dotty swallowed, and said, "It's a bidder's number."

The constable placed the bag on the green leather desk top and Dotty flattened it out. One end was torn, and the other had a dark stain across it.

Reluctantly, Dotty continued. "I wrote it for someone at the auction today, so they could bid." She twisted the bag around. "But I'm afraid I haven't been very clear. It could be an 89, or 68." She studied the contents of the bag again, before adding, "but as the paper's torn, it could also be 168, 268, or 368, but I don't think we've gone beyond 300 bidders."

The inspector joined them, and once again, Dotty felt intimidated by his presence. She stuttered, "Would you like me to look the numbers up?"

"Crackin'," replied the inspector.

Dotty tapped keys and gasped. She thought she'd recognised the first number. "89 belongs to Mrs Devereux, Aunt Beanie."

"Does it now?" The inspector pursed his lips together.

"68 belongs to a Scott Jefferies, who lives in Cirencester. Shall I print his details?"

"Oh, yes please," enthused Constable Varma, and in her excitement, she knocked Dotty's pile of green auction sheets to the floor. "Oh, toda."

As the constable bent down to pick up the papers, Dotty tapped her keyboard. "168 and 268 were new registrations today." She tapped another key. "Oh, 168 was Colonel Sutherland, commanding officer of my late husband's regiment, and 268 was Norman Climpson. I remember he arrived late and was interested in bidding for the fishing set."

Inspector Evans rocked back. "That is interesting, that is. Three of those people are also on my suspect list for the murder of Todd Mountebank. I need to have a private word with each of them, I do."

"Ladies and gentlemen," George's amplified voice announced. "I apologise, but we are unable to complete today's auction. For lots 300 and above, we are seeking written bids. Unfortunately, the police have sealed off the end room, so you won't be able to inspect the jewellery, pictures or silverware, but I hope you've already had plenty of time to consider anything of interest. Please complete a form on the table next to the rostrum and hand it to a member of staff, or our receptionist, when you are finally allowed to leave."

"Not much hope of finding anything useful in the main auction room with all those people milling around," muttered the inspector.

"Inspector," called one of the uniformed officers. "An ambulance man gave me this note. It was in the deceased's pocket."

He handed the inspector another transparent plastic bag, which the inspector laid on the table. "Constable Varma, please read it."

Constable Varma wet her lips and read, "Dotty, I'm scared. I've seen Philip's killer. I know what I saw in Cirencester. What if I'm next? If anything happens to me, promise you'll still visit Vienna. For me. Take £5,000 from my estate to pay for it. If you read this, it's too late for me. Sarah."

The inspector considered Dotty and raised an eyebrow.

Did he think she killed Sarah? For £5,000? "I've never seen this before." Dotty struggled to speak coherently. "Sarah did suggest a trip, but only this morning, before the auction started."

"Any idea what or who she saw in Cirencester?"

Dotty slowly shook her head, which was beginning to ache. "I've no idea." Poor Sarah. Why hadn't she said anything? She was probably waiting for the auction to finish.

"I'll talk to you later, but now I'd like to speak to Colonel Sutherland," the inspector declared as he glanced across at Constable Varma.

She pulled her attention away from the note. "Yes, of course. I'll find him." She rushed off to the auction room.

"Are you sure you don't know anything else? That Sarah Roberts didn't confide in you?"

Dotty gulped. "No, Inspector. I don't." She hung her head. "I wish I did."

CHAPTER TWENTY-NINE

"So, Mr Sutherland," began Inspector Evans. He was sitting on the grey sofa in the auction house reception area.

"Colonel," corrected Colonel Sutherland, sitting down opposite the inspector.

Inspector Evans smiled sardonically. "Colonel. You have blood on your hands."

Nonplussed, the colonel responded, "I'm a solider, and I've been to war."

Dotty pursed her lips. Had the inspector been trying to catch Colonel Sutherland out? Make him look at his hands or something?

"And when, in your opinion, is it acceptable to kill someone?"

Colonel Sutherland flinched but replied, "In self-defence, to protect others and for a just cause."

"And have you killed anyone in cold blood?"

"Inspector, these are not appropriate questions for a soldier. All my actions are documented in my military records."

"Quite so." The inspector leaned back, and he appeared to be sizing up his adversary. Dotty was transfixed by the exchange between the two men.

"Humour me, and empty your pockets," requested the inspector.

Dotty couldn't see the colonel's response, but she heard items fall onto the table and watched the inspector scrutinise them.

"No bidder number," commented the inspector.

"I must have left it with my auction catalogue."

"And where were you during the auction?"

"Standing by the wall on the right-hand side of the room, between the cafe area and a pair of double doors."

"And did you see Sarah Roberts?"

"I'm not sure. What does she look like? Is that the dead woman?"

"It is," replied the inspector slowly. "Did you see anyone enter or leave the room at the farthest end of the auction room?"

"The one with the valuable items being auctioned today?"

The inspector nodded.

"Plenty of people wandered in and out. I think the only person I noticed leave that room once the exciting part of the auction started was an elderly man, who was using his white handkerchief to mop up blood on his hand."

The inspector's eyes widened, but just for an instant. "Was he now? I'll need to speak to him."

The colonel stood up. "Inspector, this is an unfortunate business, but I'm needed back at my barracks. If you have any further questions, you know where to find me."

He turned and approached Dotty as the inspector looked on silently.

"Dotty, one of the sergeants found some additional boxes of items in the regimental stores which need adding to the inventory. I'm not sure there is anything particularly valuable in them, but could you call around to my office tomorrow to record their contents?"

Dotty wet her lips. "Yes, sir. Although I'll need to double check it's OK with David Rook."

"Of course."

The inspector was still staring at the closed front door, through which Colonel Sutherland had left, as Constable Varma and Norman Climpson entered the office from the auction room. Norman's head was bowed, and he fidgeted with his hands, which were clasped in front of him.

"Sir, I've found Mr Climpson."

The inspector stood up.

Gilly appeared from the auction house. "Norman, you forgot this." She handed him a foil packet. "Thank you for all your help, and I hope you hand heals quickly. We really need to sort that rogue nail, but without a porter, jobs like that don't get done," she gushed. "Maybe you should apply for the position." She laughed and turned to leave.

"What nail?" barked the inspector.

Gilly turned back and reddened. "Norman was injured by a nail sticking out of a cupboard in the far room, when I asked him to fetch me some more napkins. He cut his hand rather badly on it." She turned and scuttled into the auction room.

"Let me see?" instructed the Inspector

Slowly, Norman held out his hand.

"Nasty," observed Inspector Evans. "It must have bled."

"It did," agreed Norman. "But I always carry a hanky, which I used to stem the blood."

"Can I see?"

Norman pulled a bloodstained white handkerchief out of his pocket.

"Constable, bag this."

Constable Varma held open another transparent plastic bag into which Norman dropped the handkerchief.

"And what other items do you always carry around?" the inspector asked in a tone which was almost conversational.

Norman replied brightly, "Besides my keys and wallet, I usually have a pen, my knife and some bits of string or other items I pick up. Why?"

The inspector's eyes widened. "A knife. I'd like to see that."

"Sure." Norman fished in his trouser pocket and removed a robust looking Swiss Army knife.

The inspector leaned forward to view the knife and commented, "I take it, it is has some sharp blades?"

"Very," agreed Norman. "What use is a blunt knife? Why, on the way here I had to put a rabbit out of its misery after it had been hit by a vehicle. Its leg was broken, the poor creature."

"And which blade did you use for that?"

"This one," indicated Norman.

The inspector straightened up and asked, "Do you agree with killing creatures?"

"Sometimes it needs to be done, like that rabbit. The Duke once took a fancy to keeping chickens, but they kept being attacked by a fox. I put out some traps, but a hedgehog screamed so pitifully when its leg was caught in one that we removed them all. Two weeks later, the fox killed all the chickens, so that was the end of that."

The inspector wrinkled his nose. "Was there something you wanted to bid for today?"

"What? Oh yes. The fishing set," stumbled Norman. "And I still do." Norman glanced across at Dotty.

"So you have a bidder's number?"

"I do." Norman searched his pockets again. "I did, but I must have put it down somewhere."

"I'll see if Constable Varma can find it. Where were you sitting to watch the auction?"

"I arrived late, so at first I stood by the far wall but another customer offered me her seat in the middle of the room. It was a wooden dining chair, part of a set of six, together with a round oak dining table."

The inspector nodded to Constable Varma, who left the room.

"When you undertook your errand for Mrs Wimsey, was anyone else in the far room?"

"No," Norman shook his head. "Everyone was watching the auction. I hadn't realised how exciting it would be."

The inspector leaned back and crossed his arms.

"Have you finished, Inspector?" asked Norman.

"Yes, you can go."

Norman approached Dotty's desk and asked, "Is the fishing set still for sale?"

"What Lot number is it?"

"I'm not sure, but I think I can find it." Norman picked up an auction catalogue from Dotty's desk and flicked through it. "Here it is. Lot 371. But it doesn't have an estimated value. How much should I offer?"

Dotty drew her eyebrows together. "I'm afraid I've no idea, but I don't think it'll make a lot." She tapped her keyboard. "And we haven't received any other bids yet."

"How about £65? It's worth that just for the rods."

"I'll put that on the system, but you'll need to fill in a proxy bid form."

As Norman completed the form, Constable Varma returned and Dotty heard her say to the inspector, "I couldn't find the bidder number, but someone has been clearing up through there."

The inspector grunted as the door from the auction room opened and the people who had attended the auction streamed through the reception area, leaving via the front door. A few handed Dotty completed bidding forms. In general, they were subdued and only a few of them spoke.

They probably just want to get home, thought Dotty. Like me.

CHAPTER THIRTY

On Friday morning, Dotty was relieved not to be starting her working day at the auction house. David had agreed to Colonel Sutherland's request that she visit his office and document the additional boxes of items which had been found in the regimental stores.

Nervously, Dotty knocked on the colonel's door.

"Enter."

As she stepped inside the office, the colonel was opening a brown envelope with an impressive-looking dagger. Its ornate black handle had a thistle emblem, although she noticed it was missing from the reverse side.

"Excellent, Dotty." Colonel Sutherland stood up, walked towards a long sash window and indicated towards three cardboard boxes stacked beside it. "I apologise for not finding these earlier, but you know what our stores are like."

Dotty had no idea, but she remained silent.

"We've spent over a week looking for a boat which is listed as regimental property. How can we mislay something that conspicuous?" He shook his head.

"I've no idea," mumbled Dotty.

"Quite so. I'll let you get to work. Tea or Coffee?"

"Tea would be nice." Dotty doubted there would be a herbal option and decided to accept what she was given.

She lifted the top box down onto the floor and started removing silver-plated dishes, bowls and cutlery, which she placed on the red office carpet.

The door opened, and she heard scampering feet. A wet nosed spaniel rushed up to her and tried to lick her face.

"Hello, there. I'm afraid I don't have anything for you."

"Here's your tea," called a female voice.

Dotty stood up and took the cup from a plump, curly-haired lady.

"Thank you," she replied.

There was a yelp behind her, and she saw the spaniel dart for the door as Colonel Sutherland returned to his desk.

"Tell Williams that his dog will be banned from barracks if it appears in my office again."

"Yes, sir," replied the plump lady, and she left the office.

Dotty returned to her work, but she couldn't help wondering if the colonel had deliberately kicked or hit the dog. Poor thing, and it had been so innocent and friendly.

The phone rang and Dotty heard the Colonel answer, "Good morning, Brigadier."

The conversation started politely, but the colonel sounded increasingly agitated and remarked, "With respect, sir, I don't think that's the best course of action."

There was a long pause, before the colonel spoke again. "Yes, sir. I will." He replaced the receiver.

Dotty was soon aware of his presence beside her as he leaned against the office wall and remarked, "In a way, I'm pleased your husband isn't here to see this. He was fiercely proud of the regiment, as am I. But my job finishes once the regiment moves to Scotland, which is why it's important to make sure everything is protected, and that includes you, Dotty."

She looked up at him as he continued, "You are part of the regimental family and I will do everything in my power to keep you safe. Ian Puck has found you a nice little terraced house, at the end of a row, with a small garden. I hope you'll be happy there."

He pushed himself off the wall. "I better relay the Brigadier's news to the rest of the battalion headquarters."

As he left the office, Dotty breathed out in relief, but her stomach was still clenched. The colonel was so sure she was moving with the regiment to Scotland, but she really wasn't sure she wanted to go.

But how could she tell him? She stood up and sipped her tea, but it tasted sour.

Needing some air and space to think, she left the office and walked across the car park at the rear of the headquarters building.

As she walked through the gate onto the edge of the golf course, she spotted two players trundling their wheeled golf bags in front of them.

It had been cold the previous night and as she ran her finger along part of the chain-linked fence, she felt the cool dampness of lingering frost.

Her phone rang. Was she being summoned back to the CO's office already?

She looked at the screen and closed her eyes. "Hi, Dad."

"Dotty, are you all right? You must come home straight away. That place you work at isn't safe."

"So you've seen the news?"

"Yes, and I've spoken to Ian Puck. And he said the commanding officer was at the auction when it happened?"

"That's right, he was. But nobody saw anything, and we don't know what happened."

"Well, that doesn't matter. I've discussed everything with Ian and he'll drop some boxes around this weekend so you can pack up the house and come home until everything is moved."

Dotty's stomach churned, and she leaned against the damp fence.

"Dad, this really isn't any of your business. I have to decide when and where I'm moving."

"You've made it very clear you're not coming back here to live." Her father sounded affronted. "But I understand Ian has reserved you a nice little terrace house with the rest of the families."

There was no point arguing. Her father refused to listen.

"Look, Dad, I have to get back to work."

"Are you sure?"

"Yes, I'm working in Colonel Sutherland's office this morning."

"That'll be safe. I'll call you over the weekend."

Please don't, Dotty thought, but just replied, "Bye."

Dragging her feet, Dotty went back to her work.

CHAPTER THIRTY-ONE

Dotty returned to Akemans at lunchtime on Friday, and she had just made herself a cup of herbal tea, and taken her sandwiches out of her basket, when Constable Varma entered the office. The constable immediately eyed Dotty's lunch.

Luckily, Dotty had made her cheese speciality, with celery and tomato chutney. She'd been looking forward to the sandwiches but knew she'd still enjoy the chicken ones, with coronation sauce.

Sidling up to Dotty's desk, Constable Varma confided, "If I update you on the case, can I have one of your yummy sandwiches and a cup of tea?"

Dotty brightened. That seemed a fair exchange.

They settled down on the grey sofa and chairs, each with a cup of tea. Dotty opened the foil packet of sandwiches and handed the constable a plate, as she asked, "How is Inspector Evans?"

"Like a bear with a sore head. When he first heard there was another body, he was delighted. 'Crackin'' was the word he used, especially as Sarah Roberts' death removed one of his suspects. But he is flummoxed - that's his word - that there are no witnesses."

Dotty was about to bite into her sandwich, but she put it down on her plate.

Constable Varma reached across. "I'm sorry. Are you still upset about Sarah?"

Dotty nodded and felt a tear in the corner of her eye. "I think she understood me, and she was helping me see myself. We were both married to men who controlled our lives. I can see that now but, sadly, our husbands' deaths gave us the chance to start a fresh. Sarah through her husband's money so she could travel the world, and me, well I have some money from Al's pension, but I now have the freedom to make my own decisions."

She paused, thinking of her earlier conversations with her father and Colonel Sutherland. "If I choose to make them."

Constable Varma finished her mouthful and admitted, "My family was furious when I joined the police force. Don't get me wrong, they were happy for me to work, but they wanted me to be a doctor or dentist, not a police officer."

"Are you happy with your choice?" Dotty asked, picking her sandwich up again.

Constable Varma smiled. "I am. Cases like this one are exciting." She looked at Dotty and composed her face. "But tragic. What I enjoy most is being with local people and going to village events. I loved reading Enid Blyton books when I was a girl and the Cotswolds are just how I imagined her England to be."

"But with a few less lashings of ginger beer." Dotty smiled slowly.

The constable raised her eyebrows. "You'd be surprised what concoctions get brewed around here."

Dotty thought of Aunt Beanie and her damson gin.

Constable Varma continued, "And they still hold village shows and fetes, with classes for the best Victoria sponge, or five runner beans. And the children dress up as pirates and princesses or run three-legged races. It wasn't like that for me as a kid."

Dotty offered the constable another sandwich and asked, "What happens when you're promoted? Will you have to move to another area?"

"I could look for a sergeant's position at another station, but I like Cirencester, so I'm happy to wait. There should be a space on Inspector Evans' team next year which I'm thinking of applying for."

Dotty's smile widened. "That's great. And I doubt there'll be a rush of applicants to work with the inspector."

Constable Varma looked down at her sandwich. "There's a rumour they'll bring in a fast-track graduate from another division." She bit into her sandwich and smiled up at Dotty. "But we'll see," she mumbled through her mouthful.

Dotty leaned back on the sofa as the front door opened and Aunt Beanie entered. Spotting Dotty, she walked across and sat down in the spare chair next to Constable Varma.

"Taking a break?" she asked and, without waiting for a reply, added, "So am I."

"We were just discussing Constable Varma's work, and her future."

Aunt Beanie turned to the constable and enquired, "As a police officer?"

Constable Varma pulled her knees together and pursed her lips. "Actually, I'd love to run a little shop in the Cotswolds."

"Really?" replied Dotty, leaning forward. "And what would you sell?"

"You know me," Constable Varma blushed, "it would be an eclectic mix. Some local crafts, bric-a-brac I'd pick up at car boot sales." She added dreamily, "And there would be tables and chairs outside for a cafe, serving simple but fresh food, and a deli selling local produce."

"What a lovely idea," said Aunt Beanie, placing her hand on the constable's arm.

"Did you really set up Akemans?" asked Dotty.

"With my brother, Marmaduke, George and Gilly's father. Those were exciting times."

Constable Varma finished her mouthful and asked, "Do you miss it?"

"Sometimes, but it is different now. So many rules and regulations. It was time for the younger generation to take over."

"But you worked for Gloucestershire's Art and Antiques unit," continued Dotty.

"That was great fun. Art and antique theft is rarely a one-off event, and there are international gangs involved. But when our farmhand retired, Cliff needed my help, and I realised that the unit was unlikely to survive much longer. But I don't know what we'll do with the farm next year. Cliff isn't up to it and apart from a few animals I've cared for, farming has never been my area of expertise."

"Why don't you sell up?" asked Constable Varma.

"Oh, I can't do that. The farm's been in Cliff's family for centuries."

"Do you have any children?" asked Dotty.

"To leave the farm to? No, but I'm hoping Gilly's Thomas might take it over. He appears interested in animals and nature. George's two kids have far grander ideas than working on the land."

Constable Varma wiped her hands and turned to Aunt Beanie, bumping into the coffee table as she did. The two cups rocked, and some tea sloshed onto the table.

"Oh, toda," exclaimed the constable.

"Don't worry, I'll clear it up." Dotty screwed up the empty foil sandwich packet.

She was about to stand when Constable Varma said to Aunt Beanie, "I'm glad you're here. The inspector wanted me to ask you some more questions about Remembrance Sunday."

Dotty remained in her seat and Constable Varma looked at her and confided, "I interviewed the minibus driver from Ravenswick Hall, who was on duty that day. Sarah Roberts didn't leave on the bus at 3 o'clock, as she told us. They waited 20 minutes for her and when she did get to the bus, she was panting. The driver said he saw her hurrying up Dyer Street, towards the minibus, which was parked outside the Corn Hall."

"Oh, I saw that minibus," exclaimed Aunt Beanie, "When Norman and I returned from our walk."

"What else did you see?"

"Nothing." Aunt Beanie blushed. "I just needed a little air after lunch, before I returned to the church stall, and Norman was a gentleman and accompanied me."

Dotty narrowed her eyes. She instinctively knew the older woman was lying. "Are you trying to protect Norman?" she asked.

Aunt Beanie's eyes widened as she stared at Dotty. "How did you know?"

"I didn't, but you were being evasive, so I suspected you were protecting someone, and that it was Norman."

"He's such a lovely man. The old-fashioned type that society ignores. He's hardworking and loyal, and I don't want to get him into any trouble."

"Tell me what happened," pressed Constable Varma. "You know it'll come out, eventually. It always does." Her lips narrowed.

"Alright." Aunt Beanie rubbed her hands on her trousers and began, "Norman and I went for a short walk, as I've explained. We turned right out of the Corn Hall and wandered down Market Place to where it meets Dyer Street. Outside the lane which leads to the Woolmarket, we spotted the officer who you'd waved to at lunch, Dotty."

"Captain Ward?" enquired Dotty.

"I think so, and Norman said there was something familiar about the man, so he started talking to him. I suddenly felt Norman bristle, and he started questioning the officer about his medals. I'm not sure what the issue was, but he mentioned Korea, and something about the man being too young to have a certain medal, and another was missing. Norman became very agitated. He accused the officer of being an imposter, and they got into a scuffle. It was all rather ungentlemanly, and I had to pull Norman away. But the officer just brushed his jacket down and apologised for the mistake."

"Did Norman say anything else to the officer?"

"He didn't get the chance, as I pulled him away, back down Market Place. We did bump into another army officer. I think he might have been the one in charge, as we walked back towards the Corn Hall. He asked Norman if he was alright as Norman was still flustered and red in the face, and Norman blurted out that the man he'd just met was impersonating an officer, and he didn't know anything about Korean campaign medals."

"Who do you think the second man was? Colonel Sutherland?" asked Constable Varma.

"I'm not sure," confessed Aunt Beanie.

Dotty added, "The colonel's tall with brown hair, flecked with grey."

Aunt Beanie admitted, "He was tall and had an authoritative bearing, but I've no idea about his hair as he was wearing his regimental hat."

Dotty sat back. Then she asked, "Did you see Sarah Roberts?"

Aunt Beanie replied, "I don't think so. But then I had no idea who she was until all the press coverage for this auction. I suppose she must have been around if the Ravenswick Hall minibus was still outside the Corn Hall."

"What happened next?" asked Constable Varma.

"I said goodbye to Norman, and went back into the Corn Hall to help on the church stall."

"Did you see where Norman went?"

"No."

Constable Varma sat up. "So he could have returned to Captain Ward, got into a fight and killed him."

CHAPTER THIRTY-TWO

"Dotty, thank you for working this Saturday morning." David Rook expertly steered his vintage Mercedes around a sharp bend. "We shall be busy next week picking up the pieces from Thursday's interrupted auction. At least the police have allowed us back into the end room, so Marion and Gilly can start packing the Chipping Norton collection ready for buyers to collect, or prepare items for shipping."

The instrumental music playing on the car stereo was haunting, which matched the silver, frost-laced edge of the Cotswold landscape. Only a few yellow and red leaves added a touch of colour as they stubbornly clung to tree branches.

"The executors have agreed to a pre-Christmas sale at Windrush Hall, so we shall make it a special, festive occasion with a preview drinks party and a large Christmas tree in the entrance hall."

"That sounds wonderful," agreed Dotty. "And we could use candles. Their light is softer than harsher, modern lights and they'll show off the interior far better. I know Norman has been working hard, repairing and giving the old house a facelift."

"I know, which is why I persuaded the executors to employ some painters and hire curtains and soft furnishings to brighten the place up. Akemans' estate agency arm, which is selling the estate, will conduct viewings of the house leading up to the auction, when it will look its best."

They drove between the two stone columns, past Norman's cottage and down the sweeping drive. Norman stood at the top of the stone steps at the front of the country house and watched their arrival.

"Come in, come in," he said enthusiastically, and led them through the entrance hall. The illuminated chandelier glittered and Dotty's footsteps were muffled by a huge rug laid across the stone floor. The house felt bright and warm and she noted, with a hint of sadness as she looked through the door into the drawing room, that the blue silk wallpaper had been painted over with a fresh coat of white paint, and a pair of plush blue velvet floor-to-ceiling curtains hung in the window.

In the dining room, the covers had been removed from all the paintings, and on the recently polished sideboard, an arrangement of gleaming silverware was displayed.

"You have been busy, Norman," observed David.

Norman smiled shyly. "It's a delight to see the old place come to life, even if it's only to sell it. But I feel happier now, and I'm sure the old Duke will have a good chortle, knowing the county set's only chance of seeing the house is now that he's dead."

They entered the kitchen and there was a wonderful smell of stew. Dotty noticed a jumper laid across the back of an armchair beside the log-burner in the fireplace, and various pairs of outdoor boots lined up beside the back door. "Are you living here?" she asked.

"The executors wanted to upgrade my cottage. Add insulation and install a proper heating and hot water system, as it'll make more money that way."

"So you moved in here," noted David. "Very convenient and an excellent arrangement from a security point of view."

Earl Grey leapt onto a counter and eyed the new guests. David stepped back, but Dotty moved forward and stroked his large, furry head. He purred loudly and jumped onto her shoulder.

"There he goes again," remarked Norman, shaking his head. "He's been so miserable recently, even though I've moved in. Why don't you take him with you? I know he's taken to you."

Dotty looked into Earl Grey's large, prominent eyes and wondered for a moment if he was crying.

"See what I mean," pressed Norman.

"I'd love to," confessed Dotty. "But I live in a military house and the regiment is moving soon, and I don't know where I'll be living."

Norman nodded his head. "I can sympathise with you there. I also need to find a new place to live after the auction, and a job."

David cleared his throat. "Talking of the auction. The executors have confirmed it will be a two-day sale on the afternoons of the 11th and 12th of December. I will propose viewings on the 9th and 10th, all day, and a special invite only drinks party for select buyers and clients on the evening of the 10th. What do you think?"

Norman shrugged his shoulders. "I just do as I'm told, and auctions are your business, not mine."

"And I'd like a really tall Christmas tree for the entrance hall," continued David.

"That is something I can help with. I'll find one on the estate. Talking of which, I discovered a box of Christmas decorations when I was bringing everything out of storage. Would you like to have a look?"

"I would prefer to take another walk around the house, if you don't mind. But Dotty might like to."

"Oh, yes please," enthused Dotty.

Although most of the shops had already hung up their Christmas decorations, and many were playing carols, Dotty hadn't felt her usual festive excitement. Not after all that had happened in the last few weeks.

Norman carried a large wooden crate, which he placed on the tablecloth covering the circular kitchen table. He removed the lid and stepped back.

"I've a few more things you might like to see." He disappeared through a door beside the stairs.

Wobbling slightly under the weight of Earl Grey, Dotty approached the box. Under an outer layer of shredded paper, she discovered box after box of vintage glass Christmas tree ornaments. They were mostly delicate glass baubles whose colours were softer than modern decorations, and many of them had indented glass centres which sparkled when they caught the light.

Between two boxes was a retro-looking cardboard sheet with multicoloured strands of foil, threaded through a hook at the top. She removed a strand and draped it over Earl Grey's head as he swatted at it with a paw. Dotty laughed.

"Be careful with that," warned David as he returned to the kitchen. "Tinsel and lametta, which is what those individual strands are, were made from lead in the 1950s and 60s. Make sure you wash your hands thoroughly when you're finished."

Just then, they heard wheels crunch the gravel outside and David stepped towards the kitchen window and remarked, "Now what does he want?"

"Who?" asked Dotty.

"We have the pleasure of Inspector Evans' company."

Dotty groaned, but she was torn between a desire to escape before the inspector entered the kitchen, and wanting to hang around to find out why he was at Windrush Hall on a Saturday morning. She had a sinking feeling it was because of Aunt Beanie's revelation the previous day.

Inspector Evans strode into the kitchen and came to a halt. He raised an eyebrow as he stared at Dotty. "You look at home, you do, with that enormous ball of fluff on your shoulder." She felt Earl Grey stiffen.

"It's OK," she whispered to the cat, but she plucked him off her shoulder and placed him on the floor. He sauntered across to the fireplace.

"In fact, as you continue to appear at places connected to this investigation, and you were at both crime scenes, I'll have to consider adding you to my list of suspects."

"But I didn't know Todd Mountebank," insisted Dotty.

"That's the point. Nobody around here appeared to know him, but several people were acquainted with his various guises, including you. Did you meet both Captain Ward and Count Philip?"

"Yes," stammered Dotty.

"I also met Count Philip," interjected David. "And Dotty met Captain Ward through her military association, nothing more."

Inspector Evans continued to stare at her and Dotty realised he did not think that was all. It was not the first time his mind had connected her recent widow status with the need to fill the gap left by her husband.

The heat rose in her body and placing her hands on her hips she confronted the inspector. "I was not having a relationship with the dead man. I have just lost my husband and I am not in the market for another one. In fact, I am enjoying life just fine, on my own."

"Crackin'," responded the inspector calmly.

Dotty felt a restraining hand on her shoulder as she tried to think of a retort. David whispered, "Leave it. He's just trying to rattle you."

"And I also found these," said Norman from behind the two wooden crates he carried, one stacked on top of the other. He placed them on the table but the colour drained from his face when he looked across at the inspector.

"Good morning, Mr Climpson," pronounced the inspector. "I wonder if I might have a word with you, in private," he added, turning towards David and Dotty.

David appeared unperturbed as he addressed Norman. "I'll speak to the executors about some additional heaters in the second-floor bedrooms. Dorothy will be your main contact for the sale and she will confirm the viewing dates, and which suppliers and contractors will be coming and when."

David turned to Dotty and added, "Perhaps you should also move in here if you find yourself homeless. After all, you're going to be spending a considerable amount of time at Windrush Hall over the next three weeks."

Dotty followed David out of the kitchen and was surprised to find Constable Varma loitering in the hall. "I thought you'd be with the inspector?"

"He thought he'd make more of an impact on his own," admitted the constable.

"I presume he's questioning Norman about his argument with Captain Ward, on the afternoon he died."

"Yes. I found a shop owner who also saw the altercation, and he thought he saw Norman return a little while later."

"Oh dear," groaned Dotty. "I'm sure Norman wasn't involved. He seems so gentle, honest and loyal."

"But what if he realised Captain Ward and Doctor Rash were one and the same person?" Constable Varma had a pained expression.

Dotty followed Constable Varma's train of thought. "And if Norman suspected the doctor of stealing the Duke's medals, he might have noticed the bogus officer wearing some of them, and seen red."

"Exactly." Constable Varma opened her notebook. "After Aunt Beanie mentioned Korea, I did some digging. Captain Ward was too young to have been in that war, but both Norman's father and the Duke took part. They were awarded Korea Service Medals and automatically received Korea United Nations Service Medals. Here's a photo of the two medals. Look, they're very similar." The constable removed a colour photo from her notebook.

Dotty examined the image of the two bronze medals, each with blue and white striped ribbons, but the ribbon of the medal with the United Nations symbol on the front was multi-striped.

"Was Captain Ward wearing one of these?" she asked.

"You mean Todd Mountebank."

"Sorry, I still think of him in his military persona, as that's how I first met him. I know he wore medals, but I've no idea what they represented." Dotty bit her lip and handed the photograph back to the constable.

"Yes, he was wearing the Korea Service medal, but not the United Nations one."

Constable Varma handed Dotty another photo. "Do you recognise any of these? They were items found in the vicinity of the crime scene."

Dotty automatically shook her head.

A car horn sounded.

"Sorry, I've got to go."

Dotty rushed down the stone steps, still carrying the second photograph.

When David drove between the two stone columns, and turned onto the road back leading back to Coln Akeman, Dotty studied the photograph again.

There were several objects, including a jewelled brooch in the shape of a ladybird, a gold pocket watch and a button with a thistle on it. But the item which caught her eye was an enamelled red poppy with the emblem of a sphinx in the centre. Norman had been wearing one above his medals on Remembrance Sunday.

CHAPTER THIRTY-THREE

Dotty had just arrived home on Saturday afternoon, and made herself a cup of camomile tea, when her phone rang. She did not recognise the number and answered the call with some trepidation.

"Oh, Dotty, sorry for disturbing your Saturday, but Gilly gave me your number."

"Aunt Beanie?"

"That's right. It's me, but I'm calling about Norman. Actually, about his cat, poor thing." Aunt Beanie sounded flustered.

Dotty leaned against the kitchen counter. "Please calm down and tell me what you need."

"I don't need anything, but poor Norman does. The police have arrested him and taken him to Cirencester police station."

Did they know about the enamel poppy brooch which had been found near the crime scene, or had they arrested Norman because of a lack of alternative suspects?

"Does he want me to feed Earl Grey?"

"Who's Earl Grey?"

"The old Duke's cat. Only, I don't have keys for the house."

"Don't worry, Norman persuaded the inspector to allow him to take the cat to the police station. Can you pick it up and take it home?"

Take it home. Dotty wasn't sure she wanted to bring Earl Grey here. What if he ran off into the woods and she couldn't find him?

"Better still," continued Aunt Beanie. "Pop round here on your way back for a cup of tea so you can tell me how Norman is, and if there is anything I can do."

She couldn't leave Earl Grey at the police station, especially if they were keeping Norman in overnight.

"Ok. I'll go."

"And remember to come and see us afterwards," reminded Aunt Beanie.

As Dotty finished the call, her doorbell chimed 'ding-dong'. Who could that be? She wasn't expecting any callers, not on a Saturday afternoon.

She opened the door to a sandy-haired man wearing a white polo shirt, with a company name partially obscured by the large pack of cardboard he was holding.

"Mrs Dorothy Sayers?"

"Yes."

"These are your packing boxes. The welfare office asked me to drop them off. Where shall I put them?"

Packing boxes. She was expected to start packing up her belongings for the regiment's move to Scotland. "Oh, leave them in the dining room," suggested Dotty. She just wanted them out of the way. She'd deal with them tomorrow, or next week.

It was starting to get dark by the time Dotty parked her green Skoda Fabia in the Forum Car Park, in the centre of Cirencester. She crossed the road and approached a long, modern, flat-fronted building faced with fake Cotswold stone.

She'd never been inside a police station before and she felt slightly nauseous at the prospect. Taking a deep breath, she pushed open the front door, but rather than the quiet, empty reception area she had expected, the room was full of people.

A teenage girl had her arm around the shoulder of another girl who was holding an icepack to her forehead. Two teenage boys were arguing in a corner and a third was slumped in a chair, his head bowed. Suddenly there was the sound of retching and the boy on the chair was sick.

"Oh, Tim. Did you have to?" cried one of the girls.

Dotty pinched her nose and approached the counter. The elderly policeman, standing behind a perspex panel, muttered, "over-privileged louts", as he stared across at the boy who'd just been sick.

His attention turned to Dotty and he asked politely, "Can I help you, miss?"

"I've come to see Norman Climpson." Dotty's throat was dry and her words sounded strained.

The policeman brightened. "About the cat. The inspector will be relieved. I'll call someone to take you through."

Dotty remained beside the counter as the policeman returned with a bucket and mop. After several minutes, when Dotty nearly rushed outside to be sick herself, the door next to the counter opened and Constable Varma stepped through.

"Dotty, what are you doing here?" exclaimed the constable, "And who's been sick?"

Dotty indicated with her head.

"More students from the agricultural university." Constable Varma pursed her lips.

"I've come to collect Norman's cat."

"That's a shame," giggled Constable Varma. "It's done a far better job of winding up the inspector than any of the rest of us can do." The constable entered a key code on a panel beside a second door and they stepped into a brown vinyl floored corridor.

Dotty heard loud meowing.

"See what I mean," grinned Constable Varma.

Dotty stopped and laid a hand on her companion's arm. She lowered her voice and asked, "Why did you arrest Norman?"

Constable Varma leaned forward and whispered back. "He has no alibi after he left Aunt Beanie and his poppy brooch was found in the vicinity of the crime scene. The one with the dead cat on it."

"Sphinx," corrected Dotty.

Constable Varma straightened up. "So you did recognise it. And where is my photo?"

"Sorry, I didn't mean to take it." Dotty crossed her fingers. She didn't like lying. "But David was in a rush to leave. And I only recognised Norman's poppy when we were travelling back to Akemans." She squeezed her fingers tighter. A second lie.

"Well, it doesn't matter. Norman identified the brooch as his from the same photograph the inspector had."

"We know he had a scuffle with Captain Ward. Aunt Beanie told us."

"But with a lack of other suspects, the evidence of the brooch and no alibi, the inspector arrested him anyway. Besides, Norman isn't shouting his innocence from the rooftops. Mind you, he can hardly get a word in, not with the noise that cat's making."

They heard more haunted meowing.

"I suppose we better rescue the cat. And Inspector Evans," concluded Dotty.

Constable Varma knocked on a door at the end of the corridor.

"What?" demanded Inspector Evans.

She pushed open the door and said, "Inspector, Dotty Sayers has come to collect the cat."

"You?" he accused Dotty. "Perhaps you should join this interview. At least you'll have more to say about it than Mr Climpson."

A loud meow came from a black rigid bag with a curved top, in the corner of the room. Next to it was a plastic supermarket shopping bag.

"On second thoughts, just get that cat out of here. It's doing my head in, it is."

Norman was pale, but he looked composed, almost resigned to his fate. He stared at the table and didn't greet Dotty.

She leaned down and asked, "Norman, are you OK? Can I contact anyone for you?"

Norman slowly shook his head.

"What about a lawyer?" pressed Dotty. In TV programmes the accused was always asked if they wanted a lawyer and if they couldn't afford one, the police called a duty lawyer who was either inexperienced, or flustered with too many cases to deal with.

"I've asked Mr Climpson if he would like a lawyer present," confirmed the inspector, "but he declined."

"I think you should get one." Dotty was worried. How would

Norman stand up to Inspector Evans' relentless questioning? She was certain that since the inspector had a suspect, who'd had the opportunity to kill both Todd Mountebank and Sarah Roberts, he wouldn't let him go without firm evidence of Norman's innocence.

Norman slowly shook his head again.

"Mrs Sayers," demanded the inspector. "Please collect that cat and leave."

Dotty squeezed Norman's arm, picked up the cat basket and plastic bag, and reluctantly followed Constable Varma out of the interview room.

Constable Varma took hold of the supermarket shopping bag and remarked, "At least I should be able to go home soon."

The cat basket was heavy and Earl Grey continued to meow. Dotty bent down and looked into his large yellow eyes, partially obscured by the black mesh of the cat basket. "It's OK, I'll look after you," she murmured.

She heard a metallic crashing noise and looked up. Constable Varma had dropped the shopping bag, and tins of cat food were rolling across the floor.

"Oh, toda."

As Dotty helped Constable Varma collect the tins and packets of cat food, she asked, "Why can you go home?"

Constable Varma looked up at her. "Because Inspector Evans is convinced he's caught his man."

CHAPTER THIRTY-FOUR

Dotty drove carefully into Aunt Beanie's farmyard and turned off her car headlights. Earl Grey had been quiet during the journey, perhaps calmed by the movement of the car, but as she climbed out, he started meowing again. Dotty closed the door, but she could still hear his piteous cries.

Sighing, she opened the passenger door and picked up the heavy cat basket. Earl Grey stopped meowing.

There was no answer to Dotty's knock on the farmhouse door, so she turned the handle and, finding the door open, stepped inside. She walked through the entrance and down the corridor to the kitchen, from which she heard the sound of laughter and applause. Uncle Cliff must be watching television.

She knocked on the kitchen door before opening it.

"Dotty, my dear. How was Norman?"

Aunt Beanie was sitting beside her husband at the kitchen table. Uncle Cliff did not look up as Dotty approached, but continued to stare at the game show on the television. Beside the Aga cooker, Agatha, the Berkshire piglet, stood up in her cardboard box and watched the new arrivals.

Dotty sat down at the kitchen table and placed the cat box on a spare chair, but made sure Earl Grey could see her.

Aunt Beanie leaned across and asked, "Is that Norman's cat?"

"The old Duke's actually, but Norman has been looking after him. He's been pressing me to take Earl Grey home and now he's got his wish, but if the inspector's wish is granted, Norman will be locked up for some time."

"Poor Norman. What did he say to you?"

"Nothing. And I don't think he's said much to Inspector Evans either."

"What about his solicitor?"

"He's refused to have one."

"I must rectify that. I'll call Akemans' lawyers straight away, and ask them to send someone to the police station, before the inspector browbeats Norman into making a confession."

Aunt Beanie stood up and started searching in the bookcase.

"Get out of the way, woman," shouted Uncle Cliff.

She ignored him. "Here it is." She opened a book and entered a number into the phone. While she made the call, Dotty glanced around the room. Three cyclamen plants brightened the conservatory with pink and purple flowers. Beside one was a length of black metal with two metal ladybirds climbing up it. Ladybirds.

Aunt Beanie returned to the table, followed by little Agatha. The piglet placed her front paws on the chair beside Dotty and stared into Earl Grey's cat box. The cat hissed, but the piglet made a happy grunting noise.

"What is it, Agatha?" asked Aunt Beanie.

Dotty looked from the older woman to the piglet and wrinkled her brow as the piglet repeated the noise.

Earl Grey meowed in what appeared to be a friendly tone.

Aunt Beanie patted Dotty's arm. "There you are. They're friends now. Why don't you let your cat out so he can have a stretch and some water? And he's probably hungry. Did Norman give you any cat food?"

"Yes, but I left it in the car."

"Never mind, I've some cold chicken in the fridge."

As Aunt Beanie opened the fridge, Dotty carefully unzipped the top of the cat box. She was surprised to find Earl Grey wearing a harness which extended across the top of his back, and wrapped around his neck and tummy. She unclipped the lead, which was attached to the inside of the basket, and Earl Grey jumped out.

Agatha trotted across to him and immediately continued her happy grunting noises.

Aunt Beanie placed a saucer of shredded chicken on the floor and Earl Grey darted towards it and started munching while Agatha danced happily around him.

"What a beautiful cat. Are you going to keep him?" asked Aunt Beanie, still watching Earl Grey.

Dotty felt tired, and she tucked a strand of her shoulder length hair behind her ear as she replied, "I'm not sure. It depends where I live."

"When are you moving?"

"Soon, it appears. The army delivered packing boxes today."

"So you're staying in military accommodation?"

"I'm not sure. I haven't worked it out yet."

There was a rushing sound and Dotty was distracted as Earl Grey and Agatha raced across the kitchen floor and collided with the Aga.

"I do hope the solicitor can help Norman," confided Aunt Beanie. "I'm sure he didn't kill Captain Ward or Todd what's-his-name. He's too noble and honest."

Dotty was pleased with the conversation's change of direction, but something still nagged at her. She glanced around the kitchen and noticed the ladybirds climbing their metal pole. The police photograph of items found close to the crime scene in Cirencester had included a jewelled ladybird. She looked at Aunt Beanie. The older woman had been wearing one on Remembrance Sunday.

"What is it?" asked Aunt Beanie. "Why are you frowning?"

"Do you think Norman's honourable behaviour could extend to chivalry, particularly if he thought he was protecting someone, and that someone was a woman?"

Aunt Beanie sat motionless.

"The police showed him a photograph of items which had been discovered near the ram sculpture in Cirencester, where Todd Mountebank's body was discovered. Amongst them was Norman's regimental poppy, which he must have dropped during his scuffle with Captain Ward, aka Todd Mountebank."

Aunt Beanie gasped.

"That's the main reason the police arrested him and, while you and I both believe he is innocent, he has not denied the charges to the police. And I think that's because he also recognised the jewelled ladybird brooch amongst the items in the photograph. The one you were wearing that Sunday."

Aunt Beanie's facial muscles slackened and she looked down at her hands.

Dotty had a flash of inspiration and asked, "Did you know that Reverend Simms had stolen from you before I told you?"

Aunt Beanie stared at Agatha and Earl Grey, who were conducting a friendly wrestling match and rolling about on the tiled kitchen floor. "I'm sorry. I didn't mean to deceive you. But I thought that since you discovered the thefts, in the company of a police officer, it would make it all official and I wouldn't need to say anything. I knew the soup tureen set and oval platters were missing, but I didn't know about the fish set or the carving knife and fork until you told me. And that's the truth."

She looked up at Dotty with large, protruding eyes.

Beside the Aga, Earl Grey tried to squeeze his large frame into Agatha's box. He only partially succeeded and poked out of it like a well-risen soufflé.

Dotty wasn't finished. She wanted to believe Aunt Beanie was innocent, but how had the brooch ended up near the crime scene?

Aunt Beanie continued, "And the brooch. The clasp was broken, and I nearly lost it several times that day. Don't you remember how you rescued it when we were queuing for lunch?"

That was true. Aunt Beanie could have lost the brooch when she pulled Norman away from Captain Ward, or someone else could have picked it up and left it at the crime scene.

"Did you recognise the resemblance between Captain Ward and Reverend Simms?" asked Dotty.

"No. The Reverend was a shrunken figure with his greying hair and rimless oval glasses and he was softly spoken and demure. The officer Norman was so upset with was confident, almost arrogant, and I still can't believe the two were the same person."

"But did you tell Norman about the Reverend and the stolen items?"

Aunt Beanie drew her lips together and nodded.

"So he might have added the thefts, the brooch and the Reverend together and concluded that you were involved." Dotty glanced at Uncle Cliff as he smiled in a childlike manner at the TV.

"Norman knows what it's like to care for a loved one, but the Duke is dead and he has no idea what his future holds. He knows you have Uncle Cliff to care for and a farm to run. That you're needed here."

Aunt Beanie sat up and drew her long wool cardigan about her. "I should go to the police station straight away." She turned to Dotty and asked, "Can you stay with Cliff?"

"For how long? If you confess all at the police station, they're likely to lock you up as well. The inspector might even think the two of you colluded and keep you both in for questioning. No. The only way we're going to prove Norman's innocence, and keep you both out of jail, is to work out who the real killer is."

"Do you have any idea?"

"No," replied Dotty glumly.

CHAPTER THIRTY-FIVE

O n Monday morning, Dotty was a little later to work than usual.
She'd had a splitting headache all of Sunday and had struggled
to get out of bed when the alarm sounded at six-thirty. Only a dull
ache remained, but she felt drained.

Looking up at the three-storey stone building, she wondered if she
would still be working at Akemans the following week, or whether she
would be on her way to Scotland.

David Rook stepped out of the front door of the auction house and
waved at her. She climbed out of her car as David strode across and
announced, "No need to go inside. I have to complete the inventory for
Colonel Sutherland, and I'd like your help." He raised his eyebrows
and gave her a conspiratorial look.

Dotty was not in the mood to play games. Not with Norman
Climpson still at Cirencester Police station and Aunt Beanie calling
hourly, insisting she needed to tell the police everything. No wonder
her head was starting to throb again.

She climbed into David's silver vintage Mercedes and wound the
window down. "Do you mind not playing your music today? I have a
lingering headache."

"Of course, Dorothy. Is there anything else I can do?"

"Tell me who murdered Todd Mountebank and Sarah Roberts."

"I thought a man had been arrested in connection with their deaths."

Dotty turned to David. "Don't you know? They arrested Norman Climpson after we left Windrush Hall on Saturday."

"Norman." The car slewed across the road and David expertly turned into the skid and corrected their course. "I had no idea."

"Inspector Evans believes Norman killed Todd Mountebank after the Remembrance lunch, because he recognised he was impersonating an officer. Todd was wearing at least one medal stolen from the old Duke."

"Really, but Norman comes across as an honest, decent type of man. But then, who knows what each of us is capable of when we are pushed, and have to choose between what we believe in and what is right?"

Dotty glanced across at David, who stared fixedly at the road.

They arrived at the barracks and parked behind the regimental headquarters. There was a shout from the parade square in front of the building, and the loud stamp of the whole battalion standing to attention.

"Good," remarked David. "I was told Colonel Sutherland would be busy inspecting the troops until ten, which gives me fifteen minutes to look around his office undisturbed. There are several pictures whose authenticity I am concerned about, even though the colonel gave me the paperwork. And several objects I need to check, including a decanter with a silver horse head stopper."

Outside the colonel's office, the plump lady said, "You can't go in there without the Colonel."

Dotty approached her desk and asked, "Can I have a cup of tea while we wait, and do you have any paracetamol? I've a splitting headache."

The woman's face softened. "Of course." She disappeared down the hall.

"Thank you," whispered David. "Can you stay here and if Colonel Sutherland appears, try to delay him entering the office?"

"How?"

"Ask him what he's going to do after the battalion has moved, or something like that."

David opened the colonel's office door and disappeared inside.

The plump lady reappeared, carrying a china cup and saucer. "Here you are, and I put a pill on the saucer." She looked around. "What about your colleague? Did he want something?"

"No," Dotty blushed. "He just nipped away to check something." She lowered her head and sipped the tea. It was strong and bitter and she tried not to cough.

Five minutes later, Colonel Sutherland walked up the stairs, removing his headdress.

"Dotty, that was quick. I only just told Ian I wanted to speak to you. Come in."

Before Dotty had a chance to reply, he opened his office door and ushered her inside. Dotty looked around, but there was no sign of David.

Colonel Sutherland approached his desk, where the morning's post had been stacked. He picked up his dagger and slit open an envelope. When he placed the dagger back on the table, Dotty noticed the missing thistle emblem and she was drawn back to the police photograph of objects found at the crime scene. She had thought the photo showed a button with a thistle on, but what if it was the missing emblem from the colonel's dagger?

She was still staring at the dagger when the Colonel announced, "Have you started packing? The removal company will come on Wednesday to take the beds apart. I've also asked them to disconnect your washing machine and dishwasher, as they usually expect the occupier to do that. Can you discuss with Ian Puck the hotels you'll need here, and in Scotland, whilst your furniture is being moved? I'm told the weather is clear and bright up north, with frosty mornings. It will be pretty, although not as festive as Vienna."

Dotty started. "Vienna?"

"Yes, I understand you and Sarah Roberts were planning a trip there until her untimely demise." He placed his dagger back on the desk.

"Sarah suggested it on the morning of the auction, and nobody else was in the office. How do you know about it?"

"Oh, I must have heard you discussing it." Colonel Sutherland waved his hand dismissively. Dotty scowled. "The only other people who knew about it were the police, and I doubt you heard them talking about it."

"Well, it doesn't matter. You'll enjoy Scotland, and I believe the forecast is for a white Christmas."

"I'm not going," Dotty announced.

Colonel Sutherland looked straight at her, and her stomach flipped at his cool, menacing gaze. Then he smiled. "What do you mean? Of course you are. You're part of the family, a system which fiercely protects its own. Would you give all that up and make your way unsupported? It's a dangerous place, the real world."

Once again, he gave her a hard, cold look. "Besides, what would Al have said?"

The heat rose in Dotty's face and pounding thumped inside her head. "He would have told me to be a good girl and to do as I'm told. Just as my father would, and you also seem to expect. All of you think I should be a dutiful military wife. But I'm no longer married. And I have a job here, and friends."

"Dotty, Dotty, I applaud you for finding your little job at the antiques centre and I'm sure we can find you something similar in Scotland. But it's time for us all to move on. I'm heading back to the Middle East for another operational tour, and who knows what will be in store for me there. But as long as I know my regiment is safe, I'll be content."

Dotty narrowed her eyes. "Why the rush? I thought I had until Christmas to move, so why does it have to be this week?"

"I thought it would be for the best. It will give you time to settle in before Christmas."

Dotty folded her arms. "It feels as if you're trying to get me out of the way."

This time, the look that crossed the colonel's face was pure anger.

"You are, aren't you? You want me away from the Cotswolds, away from Akemans, away from my friend, Constable Varma."

For the first time, Dotty noticed a flash of fear in the colonel's eyes.

"That's it. You don't want me speaking to the police. What are you scared I'll tell them?"

Dotty glanced down at the dagger on the desk, and the colonel lunged forward and grabbed it.

"You couldn't let it be, could you?" he announced in an icy voice. "Accept your fate like a meek little army wife, and pack up and follow the regiment. You will be moving to Scotland, either willingly," he stood and pointed the dagger towards Dotty, "or unwillingly."

The hidden door behind Colonel Sutherland's desk flew open, and David strode across to the sideboard with surprising speed. He picked up and unsheathed the curved Iraqi dagger he had examined on their first visit.

Colonel Sutherland laughed. "You won't do much harm with that thing. It's a fake."

"This," said David, rubbing his finger across the flat of the blade, "is a Persian jambiya dagger. The hilt is made from horn and the sheath is embossed gold on wood. These three stones are opals."

"But I bought it for $20. It can't be real," spluttered the colonel.

"Many treasures were lost during the war. Now, I'd be grateful if you'd stop pointing your weapon at Dorothy. I think she expressed herself very clearly, and she's not moving to Scotland. I hardly think it's a matter worth spilling blood over."

David's calm voice eased the tension in the room.

"Of course, you're right. How dramatic of me," laughed Colonel Sutherland.

"Dorothy, I think it's time for us to go. The Colonel must have a busy morning ahead of him." The telephone on the colonel's desk rang. They all stared at it.

"Are you going to answer that?" asked David politely.

"Yes, of course." The colonel picked up the phone and said hesitantly, "Hello. Good morning, Brigadier."

He was still standing and listening to the caller as David pulled Dotty out of the office. Closing the door, David leant against it.

The plump lady looked across at him with a concerned expression.

David instructed, "Call the police."

CHAPTER THIRTY-SIX

D otty lay with her eyes closed on the sofa in the reception area of Akemans auction house. A damp cloth covered her forehead and her wicker basket sat on the reclaimed-elm coffee table.

"How are you feeling?" asked Gilly in a motherly tone. "Are you sure you wouldn't like me to call Peter?"

Dotty sat up and opened her eyes. "No, it's better. I no longer feel as if needles are stabbing the back of my eyes. It still hurts, but it's a dull ache here." Dotty cupped the back of her head and rotated her neck.

"The police are taking David's statement in my office, but I expect they'll be finished soon." Gilly squatted beside Dotty and lowered her voice. "Did Colonel Sutherland really kill the man in Cirencester? And Sarah Roberts at last week's auction?"

"It appears so."

"But why?"

Dotty wrinkled her nose. "I believe he acted out of a misguided loyalty to the regiment."

Constable Varma entered the office-cum-reception area from the antiques centre. "The inspector is just finishing with David Rook," she said, as she approached Gilly and Dotty. "David's very calm and collected, isn't he? It's almost as if he's done this type of thing before."

"What? Stop a deranged killer attacking Dotty?" exclaimed Gilly.

"Perhaps he has," mused Dotty as Gilly stood up.

"I better go and help Marion. She wants to finish packing the Chipping Norton Collection today."

Constable Varma sat down in a grey tub chair opposite Dotty and asked, "Were you scared in the colonel's office?"

"Not until he grabbed his dagger. Before that, I was concentrating on linking the clues together."

"Do you think Todd Mountebank stole from the colonel or the regiment? As he did from the other suspects in the case."

"He didn't steal from Sarah Roberts," reminded Dotty.

"No, but he didn't need to, as she paid for everything."

Dotty tried to think if there was anything missing from Captain Ward's inventory, but it had only been partially completed, and surely he wouldn't have listed anything he'd taken. She remarked, "Todd Mountebank kept the stolen items in his house in boxes or on shelves marked with letters and numbers. Do you have a list of them?"

Constable Varma removed her notebook from her pocket and flicked through it. "Here we are."

"Can I see?" Dotty slowly rose into a sitting position and the cloth fell from her forehead. She turned to the constable, who handed her the notebook.

"The numbers look like dates. 04-07 could be April to July," considered Dotty.

"Or the 4th to the 7th of a month, or the 4th of July. But as we haven't worked out what the letters mean, we didn't continue with the numbers."

Dotty examined the notebook again. "The letters are in pairs, SR, BD, DD, 8S."

She pondered, "8S is the odd one out. It's like 8 Scots or 6 Scots in regimental speak."

Constable Varma cried, "Perhaps that's exactly what it is."

"But all we found on the shelf marked 8S was an old journal."

"Is that where you found it? I wasn't sure and thought it must have been with the boxes marked BD."

"BD," considered Dotty, "and the boxes contained Aunt Beanie's crockery and cutlery. BD. Bernadette Devereux."

Constable Varma slapped her thigh. "Of course, I could never say her name and as I think of her as Aunt Beanie, I hadn't made the connection."

"So that means DD is the Duke of Ditchford,"

"On the shelf where we found the medal."

"And SR, Sarah Roberts."

"Which is where you found the box containing all the race cards, menus and theatre pamphlets, which we presumed were from events they attended together. So you're right, he didn't steal from her."

"I'm not being funny, but it sounds as if you two are solving this case without me," joked Inspector Evans.

Dotty looked up as the inspector smiled broadly. Clearly, the capture of the real killer had brightened his usual grim mood.

"We've worked out what the letters and numbers mean from the wardrobe in Todd Mountebank's house," enthused Constable Varma.

"You have, have you?" He sat down.

As Constable Varma explained them to the inspector, Dotty's thoughts returned to the black book that she'd discovered on the 8 Scots shelf. Why was it significant?

"At least we have a motive for Colonel Sutherland," announced the inspector.

Dotty dragged her mind back to the conversation.

"You do?" cried Constable Varma.

"David Rook confirmed that some of the paintings in the colonel's office are fakes and he suspects some regimental items are missing. I'm waiting for one of the police officers searching the colonel's house to drop off the items he found for David to look at."

Dotty contemplated, "So Todd Mountebank, as Captain Ward, was not stealing from the regiment, but the colonel was. Why?"

"David overheard Colonel Sutherland tell you about protecting the regimental family and keeping it safe. And when I asked why he would kill someone, one of his answers was 'for a just cause'. I believe he saw protecting the regiment, and its history, as a just cause. It's amalgamating, isn't it?"

"Yes," replied Dotty. "Which means its unique history will be lost. And the colonel thought some of the regiment's silver and paintings would be sold."

"Which could be the reason he was stealing them, so they wouldn't be lost from the regiment." The inspector pulled at his chin. "The colonel was quite insistent we return a black book. Do you know what he was referring to?"

"I think so," admitted Dotty. "We found a journal at Todd Mountebank's house, but as I was looking for more valuable items, I placed it on top of another box. When Constable Varma and I deciphered the code, I realised that it had been on the shelf for 8 Scots. Captain Ward, I mean Todd Mountebank, must have taken it. But I don't understand why the book is so significant. It appeared to be a journal of sorts."

"I'll see if I can find out when I question him formally," remarked the inspector.

The front door opened and a police constable staggered in carrying a box which was familiar to Dotty.

"Where did you find that?" she asked, and turned to Inspector Evans. "I saw it in the concealed cupboard in Colonel Sutherland's office the day you discovered me loitering in there." Her cheeks blushed.

"It's one of the boxes we discovered at the suspect's house. I've two more to carry in," explained the constable.

Dotty removed a package from the box. It was a painting. As she unwrapped the protective bubble wrap, a black horse's head appeared and then a man's, wearing a First World War uniform.

"Excellent," called David from the open doorway leading into the antiques centre. "The original Tom Keating painting of an officer with a horse."

The police constable returned with another box, and was followed by Aunt Beanie and Norman, who also held a box.

As Norman placed his box on the floor, the inspector turned to him and held out a fleshy hand. "I'm sorry for detaining you, I am. But you did have motive and opportunity. I don't mean to be funny, but why didn't you deny the charges?"

"He was protecting me," interrupted Aunt Beanie, "weren't you, Norman?"

The older man coloured as he studied his feet.

Dotty removed a photograph from her wicker basket, which she handed to Constable Varma.

"I'm sorry for stealing this, and for lying." She bit her lip and realised everyone was looking at her. "But if I hadn't," she blurted, "I wouldn't have realised the significance of the other items."

Aunt Beanie leaned over the constable's shoulder and peered at the photo. "My ladybird brooch."

Constable Varma replied, "What was it doing near the crime scene?"

Dotty mused, "I'd like to think the colonel picked it up at the Remembrance lunch, meaning to give it back to Aunt Beanie. But it fell out of his pocket when he had an altercation with Captain Ward. I mean Todd Mountebank."

"Or he could have dropped it deliberately," scoffed the inspector.

"Or Todd could have seen it, taken it, and dropped it," considered Aunt Beanie. "After all, he was a thief."

Dotty cleared her throat. "And there's another item of significance, besides Norman's regimental poppy."

"The pocket watch?" suggested Constable Varma.

"No, the thistle emblem. I thought it was a button but if you check, I think you'll find it matches the one on the Colonel's dagger, or dirk, as the officers call them, and fits into the space on the handle. He had the dirk at the Remembrance parade. I remember him securing it in his sock, which is where officers wear them as part of their uniform. He also uses it to open letters in his office, which is when I noticed the missing emblem."

"Clever girl," stated David, regarding her thoughtfully.

"Dotty, dear," said Aunt Beanie. "Norman and I would like to take you to The Axeman for lunch. We've something to discuss with you."

The inspector grinned and patted his paunch. "I'm starving me. Constable, I'm going to the pub, I am. Do you want to join me?"

"Oh, yes please," she replied as she jumped to her feet and knocked over Dotty's basket.

"Oh, toda," chorused Dotty, Constable Varma and Inspector Evans.

CHAPTER THIRTY-SEVEN

The front room of The Axeman pub was warm and cosy, and Dotty sat close to the fire with Aunt Beanie and Norman.

"Norman called me from the station," explained Aunt Beanie, "to tell me he'd been released. So I agreed to collect him, but before I left, Gilly rang to say you and David had apprehended Colonel Sutherland. So Norman and I want to thank you."

Dotty's face burned, and not just from the heat of the fire. She stuttered, "There's no need."

"There's every need," retorted Aunt Beanie. "You were right. Until the real killer was apprehended, the police would have continued to suspect Norman or myself, or both of us." She looked fondly across at Norman, who sipped his pint of Wiltshire Gold beer appreciatively.

Dotty could smell steak and kidney pie. "That's crackin', that is," she heard Inspector Evans say in his deep, melodic voice.

"There is one thing that confuses me, Dotty," said Aunt Beanie, drawing her back to the conversation, "and that's the issue of where you're going to live. Is it true you have to give up your house when the regiment moves to Scotland?"

"It is," replied Dotty as she picked up her glass of sparkling water.

"So, are you going to Scotland as well and leaving us?"

"Ian Puck, the welfare officer, has been pushing me to, and so was the Colonel."

Aunt Beanie scoffed.

"I know. I'm sure they both meant well, at first anyway, but their belief that they are supporting and protecting me is actually another way of controlling me, just as Alasdair, my late husband did."

"That's fairly typical of military wives. Give up your independence, your work and follow your husband, and in return you are given a house and your husband has a secure income and pension," noted Norman sagely, as he lifted his glass of beer to his lips.

"Well, you're not married to the army now, and it's time to make your own decisions. Starting with where you are going to live," pressed Aunt Beanie.

"And if it accepts cats. That is, if you'd like to keep Earl Grey. Beanie told me he made friends with her orphan piglet," mused Norman.

Dotty smiled. "He and Agatha were so funny. And I would love to keep him, but as you say, it depends on whether my new landlord allows pets."

Aunt Beanie stated, "I know a landlord who does, and has somewhere you can live not too far from Akemans."

"Really?" Dotty's eyes widened, and then her shoulders slumped. "But the rent around here is bound to be expensive."

"This one isn't, but it does come with some caveats."

"Of course." Dotty felt deflated.

"It might not be completely ready when you move in, as the boiler and heating system need fixing. And the decor might not be to your taste, but I'll pay for the paints if you do the decorating."

Dotty tucked a strand of hair behind her ear. "But why would you pay for the paint?"

"Because it's my cottage. Well, the farm's actually."

Dotty leaned back. "The one where the farm worker used to live?"

"Exactly. It's been empty for a couple of years, but there's plenty of space, and you even have your own garden out the back."

"And she likes animals," added Norman, nodding towards Aunt Beanie.

"Wow. That's an amazing offer."

"Isn't it just?" beamed the older woman.

A breathless Gilly Wimsey appeared beside them and asked, "Can I join you? Have you ordered?"

"You can, and we have," replied Aunt Beanie.

Gilly looked around the table. "Another pint?" she asked Norman.

"If you don't mind."

Gilly bustled across to the bar.

"I'm glad you like our proposal," repeated Aunt Beanie, "and that wasn't all we discussed in the car. The farm is too much for me to manage on my own. We coped this year by hiring some extra hands, but Uncle Cliff was still able to manage things. I'm afraid his condition has deteriorated to the point where he no longer can. So Norman has persuaded me to contract out the arable farming. It's the right thing to do and I'll still receive some money, but I won't have the worry or stress."

"Quite right," agreed Norman.

Aunt Beanie looked across at Norman as Gilly handed him a pint before dragging a spare chair towards their table.

"Also," Aunt Beanie paused, "Norman is coming to live with us, so he can help me take care of Cliff."

"We're going to buy some rare breed animals, and a Jersey cow. I've always wanted fresh milk each morning," Norman revealed.

Aunt Beanie drew her eyebrows together. "What do you know about milking?"

"Nothing, but I've discovered you can learn nearly everything on YouTube."

Aunt Beanie raised her eyes to the ceiling and shook her head. "Anyway, Norman can help around the place and do some repairs and maintenance."

"Oh dear," moaned Gilly.

They all turned to look at her.

Aunt Beanie's eyes narrowed. "Is there something wrong with that?"

Gilly shook her head. "Not at all, just David suggested we employ Norman as our porter. Apparently, he's done a great job preparing Windrush Hall for the upcoming sale."

Norman sipped his pint, but Dotty could tell he was smiling.

"Can't he do both? Do you need him to work full time at Akemans?"

Gilly looked at Norman and asked, "What do you think?"

"A house and two jobs. What else can a man ask for?" and this time Norman's grin was clear for all to see.

CHAPTER THIRTY-EIGHT

Dotty stood beside a large Christmas tree in the entrance of Windrush Hall. The delicate antique baubles twinkled in the candlelight.

She felt self-conscious in a dark blue, vintage velvet dress that she'd bought from a concession at the Cirencester Antiques Centre. She had tried on a pair of matching high heel shoes but opted for a flat pair since she was working.

"Mr Chapman, I'm delighted you could come," she greeted the Gainfords of London representative as he walked through the large front door. "May I take your coat? And would you like champagne, or perhaps something softer to drink?" She indicated towards a waiter holding a tray of drinks.

She hung Mr Chapman's coat on a hanging rail behind her as she heard him remark, "Beautiful. Absolutely stunning."

"It is, isn't it?" replied Dotty as she turned around.

Mr Chapman plucked a champagne flute from the tray and regarded her over the top of his glass. She felt herself blushing.

"Gilmore," cried George Carey-Boyd. "Don't loiter here. Come through into the dining room. I have to show you this Gainsborough painting."

Dotty checked her list of visitors for the VIP drinks reception. Tomorrow, they would begin auctioning the contents of Windrush Hall. She greeted a middle-aged couple and, after offering them a drink, she ushered them into the drawing room.

As she hung up the lady's shawl, she knocked a magazine out of the pocket of Mr Chapman's coat. Bending down to pick it up, she noticed the photograph of a curved dagger, which she thought she recognised. She opened the magazine and held it up to a candle as she read, 'Persian jambiya dagger returned to the Baghdad Museum of Antiquities." The article stated that the priceless dagger, which had been lost during the war in 2003, had recently been returned to the museum. Its gold embossed sheath and horn hilt, studded with opals, would be on display to the public in the New Year.

It looked just like the dagger in Colonel Sutherland's office. She thought David had invented its rare antiquity status to distract the Colonel, but now she wasn't so sure. And if it was part of the Colonel's private collection, how had it been returned to Iraq when the colonel had been transported directly from police custody to prison?

She felt someone watching her and looked up as David Rook, accompanying a man in Arab dress, descended the stairs. He winked at her before entering the drawing room.

Now what was that about?

Will Dotty move into Aunt Beanie's cottage and what is David Rook up to? Click the QR Code to find out in the book 2, Valued for Murder.

An antiques show. A dead diva. For an amateur sleuth the truth is not always crystal clear.

Or visit VictoriaTait.com to buy Valued for Murder.

Did you wonder why Dotty was suffering from a head injury, and what happened before she joined Akemans?

Find out in the prequel, *Hour is Come*, when you sign up to my newsletter for updates.

Hour is Come is FREE to download at
www.bookfunnel.victoriatait.com/hs6uypfw34

Why was Colonel Sutherland so concerned about the black book?

Some British Army regiments kept (and some may still keep) a record of the misdemeanours and offences a commanding officer perceives the officers under his command have committed.

It was kept secret and passed from one commanding officer, or regimental adjutant, to the next in office.

If you enjoyed this book, please tell someone you know or give them this book to read!

And for those people you don't know, leave a review to help them decide whether or not to read it.

Please leave a review on the site you purchased from
For Amazon you can hold your phone over the QR Code

For more information visit VictoriaTait.com

Made in the USA
Middletown, DE
11 February 2023

24645699R00109